398.2
Mi
cop. 5

Edited by ROSEMARY MINARD

Womenfolk and Fairy Tales

Illustrated by Suzanna Klein

Houghton Mifflin Company Boston

Lower Saucon Elementary School
1200 Wassergass Road
Hellertown, PA 18055

Library of Congress Cataloging in Publication Data

Minard, Rosemary, comp.
  Womenfolk and fairy tales.

  CONTENTS: Leodhas, S. N. The stolen bairn and
the Sìdh. — Chang, I. C. The Chinese red riding hoods. —
De La Mare, W. Molly Whuppie. [etc.]
  1. Fairy tales. [1. Fairy tales. 2. Folklore]
I. Klein, Suzanna, ill. II. Title.
PZ8.M647Wo   [398.2]   74-26555
ISBN 0-395-20276-0

Copyright © 1975 by Rosemary Minard

All rights reserved. No part of this work may be reproduced or transmitted in any
form or by any means, electronic or mechanical, including photocopying and
recording, or by any information storage or retrieval system, except as may be
expressly permitted by the 1976 Copyright Act or in writing from the publisher.
Requests for permission should be addressed in writing to Houghton Mifflin
Company, 2 Park Street, Boston, Massachusetts 02108.

Printed in the United States of America

VB 10 9 8 7 6

"The Stolen Bairn and the Sìdh" and "The Lass Who Went Out at the Cry of
Dawn." From THISTLE AND THYME by Sorche Nic Leodhas. Copyright © 1962 by
Leclaire G. Alger. Reprinted by permission of Holt, Rinehart and Winston,
Inc. / "The Chinese Red Riding Hoods." Taken from CHINESE FAIRY TALES by
Isabelle C. Chang. Copyright 1965 by Barre Publishers. Used by permission of
Crown Publishers, Inc. / "Mollie Whuppie" and "Clever Grethel." From TALES
TOLD AGAIN by Walter de la Mare. Copyright 1927 and renewed 1955 by Walter
de la Mare. Reprinted by permission of Alfred A. Knopf, Inc., and of The Literary
Trustees of Walter de la Mare, and The Society of Authors as their representa-
tive. / "Mr. Fox," "Kate Crackernuts," and "Cap O' Rushes." From ENGLISH
FAIRY TALES collected by Joseph Jacobs. Published in 1902 by G. P. Putnam's
Sons. / "The Twelve Brothers." From HOUSEHOLD STORIES FROM THE COLLEC-
TION OF THE BROTHERS GRIMM translated by Lucy Crane. Published in 1966 by
McGraw-Hill Book Company as an unabridged republication of the work first pub-
lished in 1886 by Macmillan and Company. / "The Old Woman and Her Dump-
ling." From JAPANESE FAIRY TALES by Lafcadio Hearn and others. Published in
1948 by Peter Pauper Press, Inc. / "The Forty Thieves." From THE BLUE FAIRY
BOOK edited by Andrew Lang. Published in 1966 by McGraw-Hill Book Company

as an unabridged and unaltered republication of the work first published by Long-mans, Green, and Co. circa 1889. / "Three Strong Women (A Tall Tale from Japan)." From THREE STRONG WOMEN by Claus Stamm, illustrated by Kazue Mizumura. Copyright © 1962 by Claus Stamm and Kazue Mizumura. Reprinted by permission of The Viking Press, Inc. / "The Husband Who Was to Mind the House" and "The Three Sisters Who Were Entrapped Into a Mountain." From A COLLECTION OF POPULAR TALES FROM THE NORSE AND NORTH GERMAN (by Peter Christian Asbjörnsen and Jörgen Moe) translated by George Webbe Dasent. Published in 1907 by the Norroena Society. / "East of the Sun and West of the Moon." From EAST OF THE SUN AND WEST OF THE MOON AND OTHER TALES collected by P. C. Asbjörnsen and Jörgen E. Moe. Published in 1963 by The Macmillan Company. / "Unanana and the Elephant." From AFRICAN MYTHS AND LEGENDS © Kathleen Arnott 1962. Used by permission of Henry Z. Walck, Inc., and of Oxford University Press. / "The Woman Who Flummoxed the Fairies." From HEATHER AND BROOM by Sorche Nic Leodhas. Copyright © 1960 by Leclaire G. Alger. Reprinted by permission of Holt, Rinehart and Winston, Inc. / "Clever Manka." Copyright, 1920, by Parker Fillmore; copyright, 1948, by Louise Fillmore. Reprinted from THE SHEPHERD'S NOSEGAY: STORIES FROM FINLAND AND CZECHOSLO-VAKIA edited by Katherine Love, by permission of Harcourt Brace Jovanovich, Inc.

Acknowledgments

I should like to thank Julia Mazow for her valuable comments and suggestions, and I am especially grateful to my husband, Bernie, and to James Sellers for their criticism, advice, and encouragement.

TABLE OF CONTENTS

Introduction

Not long ago at a meeting of Montessori parents a young mother protested against the reading of "traditional fairy tales" to the children. She did not want her four-year-old daughter, she said, identifying with Snow White, the Sleeping Beauty, or Cinderella. Her remarks provoked a heated discussion, and I went away determined to do some thinking of my own on what I considered to be an important and frustrating issue.

For I found myself agreeing with the young woman about the unsuitability of the fairy tale heroines she had mentioned as models for today's children. After all, if you think about it, Snow White was pretty stupid to disregard the dwarfs' advice and allow herself to be duped by the stepmother-witch *three* times; and all she had to do to win the prince and live happily ever after was be beautiful. Likewise the Sleeping

Beauty. And Cinderella certainly didn't show much gumption by meekly accepting the abuse of her stepmother and stepsisters. She would still be scrubbing were it not for her fairy godmother. I mentally ran through the other popular fairy tales portraying women and girls — "Goldilocks and the Three Bears," "Little Red Riding Hood," "Hansel and Gretel," "Beauty and the Beast." I could go on at length but not a female could I find that I would want my daughters to emulate or my sons to identify with *Woman*.

On the other hand I am a great believer in the importance of fantasy and fairy tales to the educational and cultural development of the young child. I could never agree with the militant young mother that the reading of these traditional stories be stopped. To do so would be to deprive children of a part of their cultural heritage, for the fairy and folk tales we read today have existed for hundreds, perhaps thousands, of years as part of the oral tradition of earlier civilizations; and favorite folk motifs also often appear in a more refined form in classical mythologies.

Many of us, however, are also concerned today that *Woman* be recognized as a full-fledged member of the human race. In the past she has not often been accepted as such, and her role in traditional literature reflects her second-rate position. Fairy tales abound with bold, courageous, and clever heroes. But for the most part female characters, if they are not witches or fairies or wicked stepmothers, are insipid beauties waiting passively for Prince Charming.

There are, however, fairy tales which do present their women as active, intelligent, capable, and courageous human beings. Several of these stories ("East of the Sun and West of the Moon," "The Stolen Bairn and the Sìdh," "The Lass Who Went Out at the Cry of Dawn," "Unanana and the Elephant") portray young women who persevere in their searches for loved ones in spite of great obstacles and hardships, and whose intelligence, in addition to their bravery and endurance, enables them to rescue the persons they have been looking for. The heroine of Grimms' "The Twelve Brothers" endures an ordeal of silence and faces death in order to release her brothers from a magic spell. The youngest of the three sisters entrapped in the mountain, Felice of "The Chinese Red Riding Hoods," and Molly Whuppie all keep their wits in dangerous situations and through their daring save themselves and their sisters. Displaying a similar cunning and nerve, Morgiana saves her master, Ali Baba; and Kate Crackernuts releases her sister and the prince from magic spells.

Cap o'Rushes and Lady Mary, the heroine of "Mr. Fox," are strong-minded young women who take matters into their own hands and extricate themselves from their difficulties. Clever Manka and the woman who flummoxed the fairies not only display good judgment and wisdom, but also prove themselves able and capable businesswomen, and what is more, their superiority is acknowledged by their husbands. The tale of "Three Strong Women" tells of a family of delightful and unassuming superwomen.

Most females are not superwomen, of course, but ordinary human beings; thus it is appropriate that they should be represented as such in this collection of fairy tales. Both the old woman who goes off in search of her lost dumpling and the wife in "The Husband Who Was to Mind the House" are simple, unremarkable creatures. The wife quietly copes with her unfamiliar tasks while her inept husband makes a fool of himself, and the merry old woman deliberately makes a fool of herself in order to save herself. Clever Grethel is certainly no one's fool, but she does have her human weaknesses; she is a sensualist who cannot resist good food and drink and she gets herself into a jam because of it. Similarly, in "East of the Sun and West of the Moon," the girl's inability to resist her curiosity is the cause of her troubles, and Lady Mary reveals the imperfection of human judgment when her favorite suitor turns out to be the worst of villains. But neither Mary, nor the peasant girl, nor Grethel allows herself to be defeated by her weakness, for each acts with resolve to correct the unhappy situation she has created.

Some feminist readers may object that a number of the stories I have chosen conclude with the heroine's marriage. I do not accept this objection, however, as sufficient reason for excluding a story whose heroine exhibits those qualities of intelligence, courage, ingenuity, and initiative which make a woman a human being, for in all these stories it is these strong characteristics that are important to the plot. In fact, the marriage is often simply an afterthought, a tacked-on ending typical of much early literature.

It is my hope, too, that readers will consider these stories as much for boys as for girls. Men and boys as well as women and girls need to recognize that women, too, can possess those qualities that combine to make a strong human being, and that in possessing them the woman is not unsexed but becomes more womanly just as the man to whom they belong becomes more manly.

The tales that I have collected reflect a variety of cultures — Celtic, European, Scandinavian, Japanese, Chinese, Persian, and African. Some are comic, some are romantic, some tell of princesses and some of peasant girls. All, I believe, are works of literary merit, and their heroines are admirable human beings.

Rosemary Minard

The Stolen Bairn
and the Sìdh

There was a path that ran along near the edge of a cliff above the sea, and along this path in the gloaming of a misty day, came two fairy women of the Sìdh. All of a sudden both of them stopped and fixed their eyes on the path before them. There in the middle of the path lay a bundle. Though naught could be seen of what was in it, whatever it was, moved feebly and made sounds of an odd, mewling sort.

The two women of the Sìdh leaned over and pushed away the wrappings of the bundle to see what they had found. When they laid their eyes upon it, they both stood up and looked at each other.

" 'Tis a bairn," said the first of them.

" 'Tis a mortal bairn," said the other.

Then they looked behind them and there was nothing there but the empty moor with the empty path running through it. They turned about and looked before them and saw no more than they had seen behind them. They looked to the left and there was the rising moor again with nothing there but the heather and gorse running up to the rim of the sky. And on their right was the edge of the cliff with the sea roaring below.

Then the first woman of the Sìdh spoke and she said, "What no one comes to be claiming is our own." And the second woman picked up the bairn and happed it close under her shawl. Then the two of them made off along the path faster than they had come and were soon out of sight.

About the same time, two fishermen came sailing in from the sea with their boat skirling along easy and safe away from the rocks. One of them looked up at the face of the black steep cliff and let out a shout.

"What's amiss?" asked the other.

"I'm thinking someone's gone over the cliff!" said the first man. "Do you not see?"

The other one peered through the gloaming. "I see a bit of somewhat," said he. "Happen 'tis a bird."

"No bird is so big," said the first fisherman, and he laid his hand on the tiller of the boat.

"You'll not be going in! The boat'll break up on the rocks!" cried his companion.

"Och, we'll not break up. Could I go home and eat my supper in peace thinking that some poor body might be lying out here and him hurt or dying?'' And he took the boat in.

It came in safe, and they drew it above the waves. Up the cliff the two of them climbed and there they found a young lass lying on a shelf of rock. They got her down and laid her in the boat, and off they sailed for home.

When they got there, they gave her over to the women to nurse and tend. They found that she was not so much hurt as dazed and daft. But after two days she found her wits and looked up at them.

''Where is my babe?'' she cried then. ''Fetch my bairn to me!''

At that, the women drew back and looked at one another, not knowing what to say. For they surely had no bairn to give her!

At last one old cailleach went over to her and said, ''Poor lass. Call upon your Creator for strength! There was no bairn with you upon the cliff. Happen he fell from your arms to the sea.''

''That he did not!'' she cried impatiently. ''I wrapped him warm and laid him safe on the path while I went to search for water for him to drink. I did not have him with me when I fell. I must go find him!''

But they would not let her go, for she was still too weak from her fall o'er the cliff. They told her the men would go by the path and fetch the bairn to her. So the men went, and they walked the path from one end to the other, but never a trace of the bairn did they find. They searched the whole of the livelong day, and at night they came back and told her. They tried to comfort her as well as they could. He'd surely been found, they said, by a passer-by, and he'd be safe and sound in some good soul's house. They'd ask around. And so they did. But nobody had seen the child at all.

She bided her time till her strength came back. Then she thanked them kindly for all they'd done and said she'd be going now to find her bairn. He was all she had in the world, for his father was dead.

The fisherfolk would have had her remain with them. They'd long given the child up for dead, and they'd learned to love her well.

"I'll come back and bide with you when I have my bairn again," said she. "But until then, farewell."

She wandered about from croft to croft and from village to village, but no one had seen him nor even so much as heard of anyone finding such a bairn. At last in her wandering she came to a place where some gypsies had made their camp. "Have you seen my bairn?" she asked. For she knew they traveled far and wide and she hoped that they might know where he was. But they could tell her nothing except that all the bairns they had were their own. She was so forlorn and weary that they felt pity for her. They took her in and bathed her tired feet and fed her from their own pot.

When they had heard her story, they said she must bide with them. At the end of the week they'd be journeying north to meet others of their clan. They had an ancient grandmother there who had all the wisdom in the world. Perhaps she'd be able to help.

So she stayed with the gypsies and traveled northward with them. When they got there, they took her to the ancient grandmother and asked her to help the lass.

"Sit thee down beside me," the old crone said, "and let me take thy hand." So the grieving lass sat down beside her and there the two of them stayed, side by side and hand in hand.

The hours went by and night came on and when it was midnight the ancient grandmother took her hand from the lass's hand. She took herbs from the basket which stood at her side and threw them on the fire. The fire leaped up, and the smoke that rose from the burning herbs swirled round the old gypsy's head. She looked and listened as the fire burned hot. When it had died down, she took the lass's hand again and fondled it, weeping sorrowfully the while.

"Give up thy search, poor lass," said she, "for thy bairn has been stolen away by the Sìdh. They have taken him into the Sìdhean, and what they take there seldom comes out again."

The lass had heard tell of the Sìdh. She knew that there were no other fairies so powerful as they.

"Can you not give me a spell against them," she begged, "to win my bairn back to me?"

The ancient grandmother shook her head sadly. "My wisdom is only as old as man," she said. "But the wisdom of the Sìdh is older than the beginning of the world. No spell of mine could help you against them.''

"Ah, then," said the lass, "if I cannot have my bairn back again, I must just lie down and die.''

"Nay," said the old gypsy. "A way may yet be found. Wait yet a while. Bide here with my people till the day we part. By that time I may find a way to help you.''

When the day came for the gypsies to part and go their separate ways, the old gypsy grandmother sent for the lass again.

"The time has come for the people of the Sìdh to gather together at the Sìdhean," said she. "Soon they will be coming from all their corners of the land to meet together. There they will choose one among them to rule over them for the next hundred years. If you can get into the Sìdhean with them, there is a way that you may win back your bairn for yourself.''

"Tell me what I must do!" said the lass eagerly.

"For all their wisdom, the Sìdh have no art to make anything for themselves," said the old gypsy woman. "All that they get they must either beg or steal. They have great vanity and desire always to possess a thing which has no equal. If you can find something that has not its like in all the world you may be able to buy your bairn back with it.''

"But how can I find such a thing?" asked the lass. "And how can I get into the Sìdhean?''

"As for the first," the old grandmother said, "I am not able to tell you. As for the second, perhaps you might buy your way into the Sìdhean.'' Then the old gypsy woman laid her hand on the lass's head and blessed her and laid a spell upon her that she might be safe from earth and air, fire and water, as she went on her way. And having done for her all that she could, she sent her away.

The gypsies departed and scattered on their ways, but the lass stayed behind, poring over in her mind the things that she had been told.

'Twould be not one but two things she must have. One would buy her into the Sìdhean, and the other would buy her bairn out of it. And they must be rich and rare and beyond compare, with no equal in the world, or the Sìdh would set no value upon them. Where could a poor lass like herself find the likes of that?

She couldn't think at all at first because her mind was in such a maze. But after a while she set herself to remember all the things she'd ever been told of that folks spoke of with wonder. And out of them all, the rarest things that came to her mind were the white cloak of Nechtan and the golden-stringed harp of Wrad. And suddenly her mind was clear and she knew what she must do.

Up she got and made her way to the sea. There she went up and down, clambering over the sharp rocks, gathering the soft white down, shed from the breasts of the eider ducks that nested there.

The rocks neither cut nor bruised her hands and feet,

nor did the waves beat upon her with the rising tide. The heat of the sun did her no harm, and the gales and tempests held away from her and let her work in peace. True it was, the spell of the ancient gypsy grandmother protected her from earth and water, fire and air.

When she had gathered all the down she needed, she sat herself down and wove a cloak of it so soft and white that one would have thought it a cloud she had caught from the sky.

When the cloak was finished, she cut off her long golden hair. She put a strand of it aside and with the rest she wove a border of golden flowers and fruits and leaves all around the edges of the cloak. Then she laid the cloak under a bit of gorse.

Off she went, hunting up and down the shore, seeking for something to make the frame of her harp. And she found the bones of some animal of the sea, cast up by the waves. They were bleached by the sun and smoothed by the tides till they looked like fine ivory. She bent them and bound them till she had a frame for the harp. Then she strung it with strings made from the strand of hair she had laid aside. She stretched the strings tight and set them in tune and then she played upon it. And the music of the harp was of such sweetness that the birds lay motionless on the air to listen to it.

She laid the cloak on her shoulders and took the harp on her arm and set off for the Sìdhean. She traveled by high road and byroad, by open way and by secret way, by daylight and by moonlight, until at last she came to the end of her journey.

She hid herself in a thicket at the foot of the Sìdhean. Soon she could see the Sìdh people coming. The lass watched from behind the bushes as they walked by. They were a tall dark people with little in size or feature to show that they belonged to the fairy folk, except that their ears were long and narrow and pointed at the top and their eyes and brows were set slantwise in their faces.

As the lass had hoped, one of the Sìdh came late, after all the rest had passed by into the Sìdhean. The lass spread out the cloak to show it off at its best. She stepped out from the thicket and stood in the way of the fairy. The woman of the Sìdh stepped back and looked into her face. "You are not one of us!" she cried angrily. "What has a mortal to do at a gathering of the Sìdh?"

And then she saw the cloak. It flowed and rippled from the collar to the hem, and the gold of the border shone as the sea waves shine with the sun upon them. The Sìdh woman fell silent, but her slanting eyes swept greedily over the cloak and grew bright at sight of it.

"What will you take for the cloak, mortal?" she cried. "Give it to me!"

"The cloak is not for sale," said the lass. Cunningly she swirled its folds so the light shimmered and shone upon it, and the golden fruits and flowers glowed as if they had life of their own.

"Lay the cloak on the ground and I'll cover it over with shining gold, and you may have it all if you'll leave me the cloak," the fairy said.

"All the gold of the Sìdh cannot buy the cloak," said the lass. "But it has its price . . ."

"Tell me then!" cried the Sìdh woman, dancing with impatience. "Whate'er its price you shall have it!"

"Take me with you into the Sìdhean and you shall have the cloak," the lass said.

"Give me the cloak!" said the fairy, stretching her hand out eagerly. "I'll take you in."

But the lass wouldn't give the cloak up yet. She knew the Sìdh were a thieving race that will cheat you if ever they can.

"Och, nay!" she said. "First you must take me into the Sìdhean. Then you may take the cloak and welcome."

So the fairy caught her hand and hurried her up the path. As soon as they were well within the Sìdhean the lass gave up the cloak.

When the people of the Sìdh saw that a mortal had come among them, they rushed at her to thrust her out. But the lass stepped quickly behind the fairy who had brought her in. When the fairy people saw the cloak they forgot the lass completely. They all crowded about the one who had it, reaching to touch it and begging to be let try it on.

The lass looked about her and there on a throne at the end of the hall she saw the new king of the Sìdh. The lass walked through the Sìdh unheeded and came up to him boldly, holding the harp up for him to see.

"What have you there, mortal?" asked the king.

" 'Tis a harp," said the lass.

"I have many a harp," said the king, showing but little interest.

"But never a one such as this!" the lass said. And she took the harp upon her arm and plucked the golden strings with her fingers. From the harp there rose upon the air one note filled with such wild love and longing that all the Sìdh turned from the cloak to wonder at it.

The king of the Sìdh stretched out both hands. "Give me the harp!" he cried.

"Nay!" said the lass. " 'Tis mine!"

A crafty look came into the king's eyes. But he only said idly, "Och, well, keep it then. But let me try it once to see if the notes are true."

"Och, they're true enough," the lass answered. "I set it in tune with my own hands. It needs no trying." She knew well that if he ever laid his hands upon it, she'd never get it back into her own.

"Och, well," said the king. " 'Tis only a harp after all. Still, I've taken a fancy to it. Name your price and mayhap we'll strike a bargain."

"That I'd not say," said the lass. "I made the harp with my own hands and I strung it with my own golden hair. There's not another its like in the world. I'm not liking to part with it at all."

The king could contain himself no longer. "Ask

what you will!'' he cried. ''Whatever you ask I'll give. But let me have the harp!''

And now she had him!

''Then give me my bairn your women stole from the path along the black cliff by the sea,'' said the lass.

The king of the Sìdh sat back in his throne. This was a price he did not want to pay. He had a mind to keep the bairn amongst them.

So he had them bring gold and pour it in a great heap at her feet.

''There is a fortune your king himself might envy,'' he said. ''Take all of it and give me the harp.''

But she only said, ''Give me my bairn.''

Then he had them add jewels to the heap till she stood waist-deep in them. ''All this shall be yours,'' he tempted her. '' 'Tis a royal price for the harp.''

But she stood steadfast and never looked down at the jewels.

''Give me my bairn!'' said she.

When he saw that she would not be moved, he had to tell them to fetch the child for her. They brought the bairn and he knew his mother at once and held out his arms to her. But the king held him away from her and would not let her take him.

''The harp first!'' said the king.

''The bairn first!'' said the lass. And she would not let him lay hand on the harp till she had what she wanted. So the king had to give in. And once she had the child safe in her arms, she gave up the harp.

The king struck a chord upon the harp and then he began to play. The music rose from the golden strings and filled all the Sìdhean with music so wonderful that all the people of the Sìdh stood spellbound in their tracks to listen. So rapt were they that when the lass walked out of the Sìdhean with her bairn in her arms, they never saw her go. So, she left them there with the king on his throne playing his harp, and all of the people of the Sìdh standing still to listen — maybe for the next hundred years for all anyone knows.

The lass took her bairn back to the fisherfolk who had been kind to her, as she'd promised to do. And she and her bairn dwelt happily there all the rest of their days.

Sorche Nic Leodhas

The Chinese
Red Riding Hoods

"Beware of the wolf in sheep's clothing."

Many years ago in China there lived a young widow with her three children. On their grandmother's birthday, the mother went to visit her.

"Felice," she cautioned her oldest daughter before she left, "you must watch over your sisters Mayling and Jeanne while I am gone. Lock the door and don't let anyone inside. I shall be back tomorrow."

A wolf who was hiding near the house at the edge of the woods overheard the news.

When it was dark he disguised himself as an elderly woman and knocked at the door of the three girls' house.

"Who is it?" called Felice.

"Felice, Mayling, and Jeanne, my treasures, it is your Grammie," answered the wolf as sweetly as possible.

"Grammie," said Felice through the door, "Mummy just went to see you!"

"It is too bad I missed her. We must have taken different roads," replied the crafty wolf.

"Grammie," asked Mayling, "why is your voice so different tonight?"

"Your old Grammie caught cold and is hoarse. Please let me in quickly, for it is drafty out here and the night air is very bad for me."

The tenderhearted girls could not bear to keep their grandmother out in the cold, so they unlatched the door and shouted, "Grammie, Grammie!"

As soon as the wolf crossed the threshold, he blew out the candle, saying the light hurt his tired eyes. Felice pulled a chair forward for her grandmother. The wolf sat down hard on his tail hidden under the skirt.

"Ouch!" he exclaimed.

"Is something wrong, Grammie?" asked Felice.

"Nothing at all, my dear," said the wolf, bearing the pain silently.

Then Mayling and Jeanne wanted to sit on their Grammie's lap.

"What nice, plump children," said the wolf, holding Mayling on one knee and Jeanne on the other.

Soon the wolf said, "Grammie is tired and so are you children. Let's go to bed."

The children begged as usual to be allowed to sleep in the huge double bed with their Grammie.

Soon Jeanne felt the wolf's tail against her toes. "Grammie, what's that furry thing?" she asked.

"Oh, that's just a brush I always have by me to keep away mosquitoes and flies," answered the wolf.

Then Mayling felt the sharp claws of the wolf. "Grammie, what are these sharp things?"

"Go to sleep, dear, they are just Grammie's nails."

Then Felice lit the candle and caught a glimpse of the wolf's hairy face before he could blow out the light. Felice was frightened. She quickly grabbed hold of Jeanne and said, "Grammie, Jeanne is thirsty. She needs to get up to get a glass of water."

"Oh, for goodness sake," said the wolf, losing patience, "tell her to wait until later."

Felice pinched Jeanne so that she started to cry.

"All right, all right," said the wolf, "Jeanne may get up."

Felice thought quickly and said, "Mayling, hurry and help Jeanne get a glass of water!"

When the two younger ones had left the bedroom, Felice said, "Grammie, have you ever tasted our luscious gingko nuts?"

"What is a gingko nut?" asked the wolf.

"The meat of the gingko nut is softer and more tender than a firm baby and tastes like a delicious fairy food," replied Felice.

"Where can you get some?" asked the wolf, drooling.

"Those nuts grow on trees outside our house."

"Well, your Grammie is too old to climb trees now," sighed the wolf.

"Grammie, dear, I can pick some for you," said Felice sweetly.

"Will you, angel?" pleaded the wolf.

"Of course, I'll do it right now!" said Felice, leaping out of bed.

"Come back quickly," called the wolf after her.

Felice found Mayling and Jeanne in the other room. She told them about the wolf, and the three girls quickly decided to climb up the tallest gingko tree around their cottage.

The wolf waited and waited, but no one came back. Then he got up and went outside and shouted, "Felice, Mayling, Jeanne, where are you?"

"We're up in the tree, eating gingko nuts," called Felice.

"Throw some down for me," yelled the wolf.

"Ah, Grammie, we just remember Mummy telling us that gingkos are fairy nuts. They change when they leave the tree. You'll just have to climb up and eat these mouth-watering nuts here."

The wolf was raging as he paced back and forth under the tree.

Then Felice said, "Grammie, I just had an idea.

There is a clothesbasket by the door with a long clothesline inside. Tie one end to the handle and throw the end of the rope up to me. We shall pull you up here.''

The wolf happily went to get the clothesbasket.

Felice pulled hard on the rope. When the basket was halfway up, she let go, and the wolf fell to the ground badly bruised.

''Boo hoo, hoo!'' cried Felice, pretending to be very sorry. ''I did not have enough strength to pull poor Grammie up!''

''Don't cry, Sister,'' said Mayling, ''I'll help you pull Grammie up!''

The greedy wolf got into the basket again.

Felice and Mayling pulled with all their might. The wolf was two thirds up the tree before they let go of the rope. Down he fell with a crash. He began to scold.

''Grammie, Grammie, please don't get so upset,'' begged Jeanne. ''I'll help my sisters to pull you all the way up this time.''

''All right, but mind you be very careful or I'll bite your heads off!'' screeched the wolf.

The three children pulled with all their strength.

''Heave ho, heave ho!'' they sang in rhythm as they hauled the wolf up slowly till he was thirty feet high. He was just beyond reach of a branch when Felice coughed, and everyone let go of the rope. As the basket spun down, the wolf let out his last howl.

When the children were unable to get any answer to their calls of "Grammie," they slid down the tree and ran into the house, latched the door and soon went to sleep.

Isabelle C. Chang

Molly Whuppie

Once upon a time, there was an old woodcutter who had too many children. Work as hard as he might, he couldn't feed them all. So he took the three youngest of them, gave them a last slice of bread and treacle each, and abandoned them in the forest.

They ate the bread and treacle and walked and walked until they were worn out and utterly lost. Soon they would have lain down together like the babes in the wood, and that would have been the end of them if, just as it was beginning to get dark, they had not spied a small and beaming light between the trees. Now this light was chinkling out from a window. So the youngest of them, who was called Molly Whuppie and was by far the cleverest, went and knocked at the door.

A woman came to the door and asked them what they wanted. Molly Whuppie said: "Something to eat."

"Eat!" said the woman. "Eat! Why, my husband's a giant, and soon as say knife, he'd eat *you*."

But they were tired out and famished, and still Molly begged the woman to let them in.

So at last the woman took them in, sat them down by the fire on a billet of wood, and gave them some bread and milk. Hardly had they taken a sup of it when there came a thumping at the door. No mistaking that: it was the giant come home; and in he came.

"Hai!" he said, squinting at the children. "What have we here?"

"Three poor, cold, hungry, lost little lasses," said his wife. "You get to your supper, my man, and leave them to me."

The giant said nothing, sat down and ate up his supper; but between the bites he looked at the children.

Now the giant had three daughters of his own, and the giant's wife put the whole six of them into the same bed. For so she thought she would keep the strangers safe. But before he went to bed the giant, as if in play, hung three chains of gold round his daughters' necks, and three of golden straw round Molly's and her sisters' between the sheets.

Soon the other five were fast asleep in the great bed, but Molly lay awake listening. At last she rose up softly, and, creeping across, changed over one by one the necklaces of gold and of straw. So now it was

Molly and her sisters who wore the chains of gold, and the giant's three daughters the chains of straw. Then she lay down again.

In the middle of the night the giant came tiptoeing into the room, and, groping cautiously with finger and thumb, he plucked up out of the bed the three children with the straw necklaces round their necks, carried them downstairs, and bolted them up in his great cellar.

"So, so, my pretty chickabiddies!" he smiled to himself as he bolted the door. "Now you're safe!"

As soon as all was quiet again, Molly Whuppie thought it high time she and her sisters were out of that house. So she woke them, whispering in their ears, and they slipped down the stairs together and out into the forest, and never stopped running till morning.

But daybreak came at last, and lo and behold, they came to another house. It stood beside a pool of water full of wild swans, and stone images there, and a thousand windows; and it was the house of the King. So Molly went in, and told her story to the King. The King listened, and when it was finished, said:

"Well, Molly, that's one thing done, and done well. But I could tell another thing, and that would be a better." This King, indeed, knew the giant of old; and he told Molly that if she would go back and steal for him the giant's sword that hung behind his bed, he would give her eldest sister his eldest son for a husband, and then Molly's sister would be a princess.

Molly looked at the eldest prince, for there they all

sat at breakfast, and she smiled and said she would try.

So, that very evening, she muffled herself up, and made her way back through the forest to the house of the giant. First she listened at the window, and there she heard the giant eating his supper; so she crept into the house and hid herself under his bed.

In the middle of the night — and the shutters fairly shook with the giant's snoring — Molly climbed softly up on to the great bed and unhooked the giant's sword that was dangling from its nail in the wall. Lucky it was for Molly this was not the giant's great fighting sword, but only a little sword. It was heavy enough for all that, and when she came to the door, it rattled in its scabbard and woke up the giant.

Then Molly ran, and the giant ran, and they both ran, and at last they came to the Bridge of the One Hair, and Molly ran over. But not the giant; for run over he couldn't. Instead, he shook his fist at her across the great chasm in between, and shouted:

> *"Woe betide ye, Molly Whuppie,*
> *If ye e'er come back again!"*

But Molly only laughed and said:

> *"Maybe twice I'll come to see 'ee,*
> *If so be I come to Spain."*

Then Molly carried off the sword to the King; and her eldest sister married the King's eldest son.

"Well," said the King, when the wedding was over,

"that was a better thing done, Molly, and done well. But I know another, and that's better still. Steal the purse that lies under the giant's pillow, and I'll marry your second sister to my second son."

Molly looked at the King's second son, and laughed, and said she would try.

So she muffled herself up in another-colored hood, and stole off through the forest to the giant's house, and there he was, guzzling as usual at supper. This time she hid herself in his linen closet. A stuffy place that was.

About the middle of the night, she crept out of the linen closet, took a deep breath, and pushed in her fingers just a little bit betwixt his bolster and pillow. The giant stopped snoring and sighed, but soon began to snore again. Then Molly slid her fingers in a little bit further under his pillow. At this the giant called out in his sleep as if there were robbers near. And his wife said: "Lie easy, man! It's those bones you had for supper."

Then Molly pushed in her fingers even a little bit further, and then they felt the purse. But as she drew out the purse from under the pillow, a gold piece dropped out of it and clanked on to the floor, and at sound of it the giant woke.

Then Molly ran, and the giant ran, and they both ran. And they both ran and ran until they came to the Bridge of the One Hair. And Molly got over, but the giant stayed; for get over he couldn't. Then he cried out on her across the chasm:

"Woe betide ye, Molly Whuppie,
If ye e'er come back again!"

But Molly only laughed, and called back at him:

"Once again I'll come to see 'ee,
If so be I come to Spain."

So she took the purse to the King, and her second sister married his second son; and there were great rejoicings.

"Well, well," said the King to Molly, when the feasting was over, "that was yet a better thing done, Molly, and done for good. But I know a better yet, and that's the best of all. Steal the giant's ring for me from off his thumb, and you shall have my youngest son for yourself. And all solemn, Molly, you always were my favorite."

Molly laughed and looked at the King's youngest son, turned her head, frowned, then laughed again, and said she would try. This time, when she had stolen into the giant's house, she hid in the chimney niche.

At dead of night, when the giant was snoring, she stepped out of the chimney niche and crept towards the bed. By good chance the giant lay on his back, his head on his pillow, with his arm hanging down out over the bedside, and it was the arm that had the hand at the end of it on which was the great thumb that wore the ring. First Molly wetted the giant's thumb, then she tugged softly and softly at the ring. Little by little it

slid down and down over the knuckle-bone; but just as Molly had slipped it off and pushed it into her pocket, the giant woke with a roar, clutched at her, gripped her, and lifted her clean up into the dark over his head.

"Ah-ha! Molly Whuppie!" says he. "Once too many is never again. Ay, and if *I'd* done the ill to you as the ill you have done's been done to me, what would I be getting for *my* pains?"

"Why," says Molly all in one breath, "I'd bundle you up into a sack, and I'd put the cat and dog inside with you, and a needle and thread and a great pair of shears, and I'd hang you up on the wall, be off to the wood, cut the thickest stick I could get, come home, take you down, and beat you to a jelly. *That's* what I'd do!"

"And that, Molly," says the giant, chuckling to himself with pleasure and pride at his cunning, "that's just what I will be doing with you." So he rose up out of his bed and fetched a sack, put Molly into the sack, and the cat and the dog besides, and a needle and thread and a stout pair of shears, and hung her up on the wall. Then away he went into the forest to cut a cudgel.

When he was well gone, Molly, stroking the dog with one hand and the cat with the other, sang out in a high, clear, jubilant voice: "Oh, if only everybody could see what I can see!"

" 'See,' Molly?" said the giant's wife. "What do you see?"

But Molly only said, "Oh, if only everybody could

see what I see! Oh, if only they could see what *I* see!''

At last the giant's wife begged and entreated Molly to take her up into the sack so that she could see what Molly saw. Then Molly took the shears and cut a hole in the lowest corner of the sack, jumped out of the sack, helped the giant's wife up into it, and, as fast as she could, sewed up the hole with the needle and thread.

But it was pitch black in the sack, so the giant's wife saw nothing but stars, and they were inside of her, and she soon began to ask to be let out again. Molly never heeded or answered her, but hid herself far in at the back of the door. Home at last came the giant, with a quickwood cudgel in his hand and a knob on the end of it as big as a pumpkin. And he began to belabour the sack with the cudgel.

His wife cried: ''Stay, man! It's me, man! Oh, man, it's me, man!'' But the dog barked and the cat squalled, and at first he didn't hear her voice.

Then Molly crept softly out from behind the door. But the giant saw her. He gave a roar. And Molly ran, and the giant ran, and they both ran, and they ran and they ran and they ran — Molly and the giant — till they came to the Bridge of the One Hair. And Molly skipped along over it; but the giant stayed, for he couldn't. And he cried out after her in a dreadful voice across the chasm:

> *''Woe betide ye, Molly Whuppie,*
> *If ye e'er come back again!''*

But Molly waved her hand at the giant over the chasm, and flung back her head:

> "Never *again I'll come to see 'ee,*
> *Though so be I come to Spain."*

Then Molly ran off with the ring in her pocket, and she was married to the King's youngest son; and there was a feast that was a finer feast than all the feasts that had ever been in the King's house before, and there were lights in all the windows.

Lights so bright that all the dark long the hosts of the wild swans swept circling in space under the stars. But though there were guests by the hundred from all parts of the country, the giant never so much as gnawed a bone!

Walter de la Mare

Mr. Fox

Lady Mary was young, and Lady Mary was fair. She had two brothers and more lovers than she could count. But of them all, the bravest and most gallant was a Mr. Fox, whom she met when she was down at her father's country house. No one knew who Mr. Fox was; but he was certainly brave and surely rich, and of all her lovers, Lady Mary cared for him alone. At last it was agreed upon between them that they should be married. Lady Mary asked Mr. Fox where they should live, and he described to her his castle and where it was; but, strange to say, he did not ask her or her brothers to come and see it.

So one day, near the wedding day, when her brothers were out and Mr. Fox was away for a day or two on business, as he said, Lady Mary set out for Mr. Fox's castle. After many searchings she came at last to it, and a fine strong house it was with high walls and a deep moat. When she came up to the gateway she saw written on it:

Be bold, be bold.

But as the gate was open, she went through it and found no one there. So she went up to the doorway, and over it she found written:

Be bold, be bold, but not too bold.

Still she went on, till she came into the hall, and went up the broad stairs till she came to a door in the gallery, over which was written:

Be bold, be bold, but not too bold,
Lest that your heart's blood should run cold.

But Lady Mary was a brave one, she was. She opened the door, and what do you think she saw? Why, bodies and skeletons of beautiful young ladies all stained with blood. So Lady Mary thought it was high time to get out of that horrid place; she closed the door, went through the gallery, and was just going down the stairs and out of the hall, when who should she see through the window but Mr. Fox, dragging a beautiful young

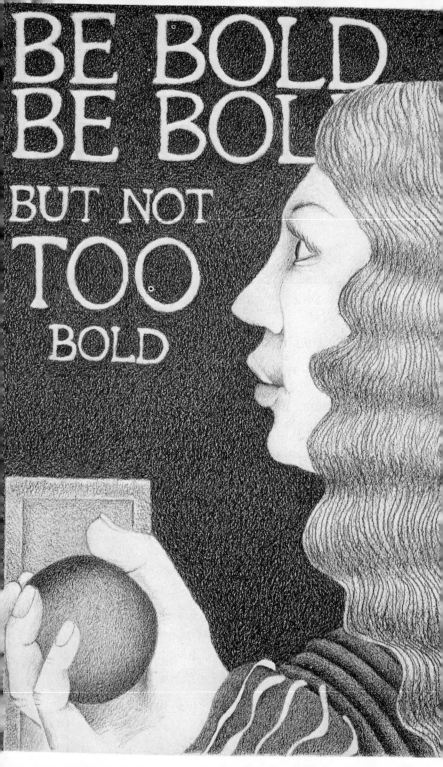

lady along from the gateway to the door. Lady Mary rushed downstairs and hid herself behind a cask, just in time, as Mr. Fox came in with the poor young lady who seemed to have fainted. Just as he got near Lady Mary, Mr. Fox saw a diamond ring glittering on the finger of the young lady he was dragging, and he tried to pull it off. But it was tightly fixed and would not come off, so Mr. Fox cursed and swore. He drew his sword, raised it, and brought it down upon the hand of the poor lady. The sword cut off the hand, which jumped up into the air and fell, of all places in the world, into Lady Mary's lap. Mr. Fox looked about a bit, but did not think of looking behind the cask; so at last he went on dragging the young lady up the stairs into the Bloody Chamber.

As soon as she heard him pass through the gallery, Lady Mary crept out of the door, down through the gateway, and ran home as fast as she could.

Now it happened that the very next day the marriage contract of Lady Mary and Mr. Fox was to be signed, and there was a splendid breakfast before that. And when Mr. Fox was seated at table opposite Lady Mary, he looked at her. "How pale you are this morning, my dear."

"Yes," said she, "I had a bad night's rest last night. I had horrible dreams."

"Dreams go by contraries," said Mr. Fox, "but tell us your dream, and your sweet voice will make the time pass till the happy hour comes."

"I dreamed," said Lady Mary, "that I went yestermorn to your castle; and I found it in the woods, with high walls and a deep moat, and over the gateway was written:

Be bold, be bold."

"But it is not so, nor it was not so," said Mr. Fox.

"And when I came to the doorway, over it was written:

Be bold, be bold, but not too bold."

"It is not so, nor it was not so," said Mr. Fox.

"And then I went upstairs and came to a gallery at the end of which was a door, on which was written:

Be bold, be bold, but not too bold,
Lest that your heart's blood should run cold."

"It is not so, nor it was not so," said Mr. Fox.

"And then — and then I opened the door, and the room was filled with bodies and skeletons of poor dead women, all stained with their blood."

"It is not so, nor it was not so. And God forbid it should be so," said Mr. Fox.

"I then dreamed that I rushed down the gallery and just as I was going down the stairs, I saw you, Mr. Fox, coming up to the hall door, dragging after you a poor young lady, rich and beautiful."

"It is not so, nor it was not so. And God forbid it should be so," said Mr. Fox.

"I rushed downstairs just in time to hide myself behind a cask, when you, Mr. Fox, came in, dragging the young lady by the arm. And as you passed me, Mr. Fox, I thought I saw you try to get off her diamond ring; and when you could not, Mr. Fox, it seemed to me in my dream that you drew out your sword and hacked off the poor lady's hand to get the ring."

"It is not so, nor it was not so. And God forbid it should be so," said Mr. Fox.

He was going to say something else as he rose from his seat, but Lady Mary cried out: "But it is so, and it was so. Here's hand and ring I have to show," and she pulled out the lady's hand from her dress, and pointed it straight at Mr. Fox.

At once her brothers and her friends drew their swords and cut Mr. Fox into a thousand pieces.

Joseph Jacobs

The Twelve Brothers

Once upon a time there lived a King and Queen very peacefully together; they had twelve children, all boys. Now the King said to the Queen one day, "If your thirteenth child should be a girl the twelve boys shall die, so that her riches may be the greater and the kingdom fall to her alone."

Then he caused twelve coffins to be made. They were filled with shavings, and a little pillow was laid in each, and they were put in a locked-up room. The King gave the key to the Queen and told her to say nothing about it to anyone.

But the mother sat the whole day sorrowing, so that her youngest son, who never left her, and to whom she had given the Bible name Benjamin, said to her, "Dear mother, why are you so sad?"

"Dearest child," answered she, "I dare not tell you."

But he let her have no peace until she went and unlocked the room and showed him the twelve coffins with the shavings and the little pillows. Then she said, "My dear Benjamin, your father has caused these coffins to be made for you and your eleven brothers, and if I bring a little girl into the world you are all to be put to death together and buried therein."

And she wept as she spoke, and her little son comforted her and said, "Weep not, dear mother. We will save ourselves and go far away."

Then she answered, "Yes, go with your eleven brothers out into the world, and let one of you always sit on the top of the highest tree that can be found and keep watch upon the tower of this castle. If a little son is born I will put out a white flag, and then you may safely venture back again; but if it is a little daughter, I will put out a red flag — then flee away as fast as you can, and the dear God watch over you. Every night will I arise and pray for you — in winter that you may have a fire to warm yourselves by, and in summer that you may not languish in the heat."

After that, when she had given her sons her blessing, they went away out into the wood. One after another kept watch, sitting on the highest oak tree, looking towards the tower. When eleven days had passed and Benjamin's turn came, he saw a flag put out; it was not white, but blood red, to warn them that they were to die. When the brothers knew this they became angry, saying, "Shall we suffer death because of a girl! We swear to be revenged; wherever we find a girl we will shed her blood."

Then they went deeper into the wood; and in the middle, where it was darkest, they found a little enchanted house, standing empty. Then they said, "Here will we dwell. You, Benjamin, the youngest and weakest, shall stay at home and keep house; we others will go abroad and purvey food."

Then they went into the wood and caught hares, wild roes, birds, and pigeons, and whatever else is good to eat, and brought them to Benjamin to cook and make ready to satisfy their hunger. So they lived together in the little house for ten years, and the time did not seem long.

By this time the Queen's little daughter was growing up. She had a kind heart and a beautiful face, and a golden star on her forehead. Once when there was a great wash she saw among the clothes twelve shirts, and she asked her mother, "Whose are these twelve shirts? They are too small to be my father's."

Then the mother answered with a sore heart, "Dear child, they belong to your twelve brothers."

The little girl said, "Where are my twelve brothers? I have never heard of them."

And her mother answered, "God only knows where they are wandering about in the world." Then she led the little girl to the secret room and unlocked it, and showed her the twelve coffins with the shavings and the little pillows.

"These coffins," said she, "were intended for your twelve brothers, but they went away far from home when you were born"; and she related how everything had come to pass.

Then said the little girl, "Dear mother, do not weep. I will go and seek my brothers."

So she took the twelve shirts and went far and wide in the great forest. The day sped on, and in the evening she came to the enchanted house. She went in and found a youth, who asked, "Whence do you come, and what do you want?" He marvelled at her beauty, her royal garments, and the star on her forehead.

Then she answered, "I am a king's daughter, and I seek my twelve brothers. I will go everywhere under the blue sky until I find them." And she showed him the twelve shirts which belonged to them.

Then Benjamin saw that it must be his sister and said, "I am Benjamin, your youngest brother."

She began weeping for joy, and Benjamin did also; they kissed and cheered each other with great love. After a while he said, "Dear sister, there is still a hindrance. We have sworn that any maiden that we meet must die, as it was because of a maiden that we had to leave our kingdom."

Then she said, "I will willingly die, if so I may benefit my twelve brothers."

"No," answered he, "you shall not die. Sit down

under this tub until the eleven brothers come and I consult with them about it.'' She did so. As night came on they returned from hunting, and supper was ready.

As they were sitting at the table eating, they asked, ''What news?''

And Benjamin said, ''Don't you know any?''

''No,'' answered they.

So he said, ''You have been in the wood, and I have stayed at home; yet I know more than you.''

''Tell us!'' cried they.

He answered, ''Promise me that the first maiden we see shall not be put to death.''

''Yes, we promise,'' cried they all. ''She shall have mercy; tell us now.''

Then he said, ''Our sister is here,'' and lifted up the tub. The king's daughter with the golden star on her forehead came forth in her royal garments. She seemed so beautiful, delicate, and sweet that they all rejoiced and fell on her neck and kissed her, and loved her with all their hearts.

After this she remained with Benjamin in the house and helped him with the work. The others went into the woods to catch wild animals, roes, birds, and pigeons, for food for them all. Their sister and Benjamin took care that all was made ready for them.

One day the two prepared a fine feast. When everyone was assembled they sat down and ate and drank and were full of joy. Now there was a little garden which belonged to the enchanted house and in which grew twelve lilies. The maiden, thinking to please her brothers, went out to gather the twelve flowers, meaning to give one to each as they sat at meat. But as she broke off the flowers, in the same moment the brothers were changed into twelve ravens, and flew over the wood far away; and the house with the garden also disappeared.

So the poor maiden stood alone in the wild wood. As she was looking around her she saw an old woman standing by her, who said, "My child, what hast thou done! Why couldst thou not leave the twelve flowers standing? They were thy twelve brothers, who are now changed to ravens forever."

The maiden said, weeping, "Is there no means of setting them free?"

"No," said the old woman, "there is in the whole world no way but one, and that is difficult; thou canst not release them but by being dumb for seven years. Thou must neither speak nor laugh, and wert thou to speak one single word — and it wanted but one hour of the seven years — all would be in vain. Thy brothers would perish because of that one word."

Then the maiden said in her heart, "I am quite sure that I can set my brothers free," and went and sought a tall tree, climbed up, and sat there spinning, and never spoke or laughed.

Now it happened that a King, who was hunting in the wood, had with him a large greyhound, who ran to the tree where the maiden was, sprang up at it, and barked loudly. Up rode the King and saw the beautiful

Princess with the golden star on her forehead, and he was so charmed with her beauty that he beseeched her to become his wife. She gave no answer, only a little nod of her head. Then he himself climbed the tree and brought her down, set her on his horse and took her home. The wedding was held with great splendor and rejoicing, but the bride neither spoke nor laughed.

After they had lived pleasantly together for a few years, the King's mother, who was a wicked woman, began to slander the young Queen and said to the King, "She is only a low beggar-maid that you have taken to yourself. Who knows what mean tricks she is playing? Even if she is really dumb and cannot speak she might at least laugh; not to laugh is the sign of a bad conscience."

At first the King would believe nothing of it, but the old woman talked so long and suggested so many bad things that he at last let himself be persuaded and condemned the Queen to death.

Now a great fire was kindled in the courtyard, and she was to be burned in it. The King stood above at the window and watched it all with weeping eyes, for he had held her very dear. And when she was already bound fast to the stake and the fire was licking her garments with red tongues, the last moment of the seven years came to an end. Then a rushing sound was heard in the air and twelve ravens came flying and sank downwards; as they touched the earth they became the twelve brothers that she had lost. They rushed through the fire and quenched the flames, and set their dear sister free, kissing and consoling her. And now that her mouth was opened and she might venture to speak, she told the King the reason for her dumbness and why she had never laughed. The King rejoiced when he heard of her innocence, and they all lived together in happiness until their death.

But the wicked mother-in-law was very unhappy and died miserably.

The Brothers Grimm

The Old Woman and Her Dumpling

Long, long ago there was a funny old woman who liked to laugh and make dumplings of rice flour.

One day while she was preparing some dumplings for dinner, she let one fall, and it rolled into a hole in the earthen floor of her little kitchen and disappeared. The old woman tried to reach it by putting her hand down the hole, but all at once the earth gave way, and the old woman fell in.

She fell quite a distance but was not a bit hurt. When she got up on her feet again, she saw that she was standing on a road, just like the road before her house. It was quite light down there, and she could see plenty of rice fields, but no one in them. How all this happened, I cannot tell you. But it seems that the old woman had fallen into another country.

The road she had fallen upon sloped very much; so, after having looked for her dumpling in vain, she thought that it must have rolled farther away down the slope. She ran down the road to look, crying, "My dumpling, my dumpling! Where is that dumpling of mine?"

After a little while she saw a stone *Jizo* standing by the roadside, and she said, "O Lord *Jizo,* did you see my dumpling?"

Jizo answered, "Yes, I saw your dumpling rolling by me down the road. But you had better not go any farther, because there is a wicked *Oni* living down there, who eats people."

But the old woman only laughed and ran on farther down the road, crying, "My dumpling, my dumpling! Where is that dumpling of mine?" And she came to another statue of *Jizo,* and asked it, "O kind Lord *Jizo,* did you see my dumpling?"

And *Jizo* said, "Yes, I saw your dumpling go by a little while ago. But you must not run any farther, because there is a wicked *Oni* down there, who eats people."

But she only laughed and ran on, still crying out, "My dumpling, my dumpling! Where is that dumpling of mine?" And she came to a third *Jizo,* and asked it, "O dear Lord *Jizo,* did you see my dumpling?"

But *Jizo* said, "Don't talk about your dumpling now. Here is the *Oni* coming. Squat down here behind my sleeve and don't make any noise."

Presently the *Oni* came very close and stopped and bowed to *Jizo,* and said, "Good day, *Jizo San!*"

Jizo said good day, too, very politely.

Then the *Oni* suddenly snuffed the air two or three times in a suspicious way and cried out, *"Jizo San, Jizo San!* I smell a smell of mankind somewhere — don't you?"

"Oh!" said *Jizo.* "Perhaps you are mistaken."

"No, no!" said the *Oni* after snuffing the air again. "I smell a smell of mankind."

Then the old woman could not help laughing — *"Te-he-he!"* — and the *Oni* immediately reached down his big hairy hand behind *Jizo's* sleeve and pulled her out, still laughing, *"Te-he-he!"*

"Aha!" cried the *Oni.*

Then *Jizo* said, "What are you going to do with that good old woman? You must not hurt her."

"I won't," said the *Oni.* "But I will take her home with me to cook for us."

"Very well," said *Jizo,* "but you must really be kind to her. If you are not, I shall be very angry."

"I won't hurt her at all," promised the *Oni.* "She will only have to do a little work for us every day. Good-by, *Jizo San.*"

Then the *Oni* took the old woman far down the road till they came to a wide deep river, where there was a boat. He put her into the boat and took her across the river to his house. It was a very large house. He led her at once into the kitchen and told her to cook some dinner for himself and the other *Oni* who lived with him.

And he gave her a small wooden rice paddle, and said, "You must always put only one grain of rice into the pot, and when you stir that one grain of rice in the water with this paddle, the grain will multiply until the pot is full."

So the old woman put just one rice grain into the pot, as the *Oni* told her, and began to stir it with the paddle. As she stirred, the one grain became two, then four, then eight, then sixteen, thirty-two, sixty-four, and so on. Every time she moved the paddle the rice increased in quantity, and in a few minutes the great pot was full.

After that the funny old woman stayed a long time in the house of the *Oni* and every day cooked food for him and for all his friends. The *Oni* never hurt or frightened her, and her work was made quite easy by the magic paddle — although she had to cook a very, very great quantity of rice, because an *Oni* eats much more than any human being eats.

But she felt lonely and always wished very much to go back to her own little house and make her dumplings. And one day, when the *Oni* were all out somewhere, she thought she would try to run away.

She first took the magic paddle and slipped it under her girdle; then she went down to the river. No one saw her, and the boat was there. She got into it and pushed off. As she could row very well, she was soon far away from the shore.

But the river was very wide; and she had not rowed more than one fourth of the way across when the *Oni,* all of them, came back to the house. They found that their cook was gone, and the magic paddle, too. They ran down to the river at once and saw the old woman rowing away very fast.

Perhaps they could not swim. At all events they had no boat, and they thought the only way they could catch the funny old woman would be to drink up all the water of the river before she got to the other bank. So they knelt down and began to drink so fast that before the old woman had got halfway over, the water had become quite low.

But the old woman kept on rowing until the water had got so shallow that the *Oni* stopped drinking and began to wade across. Then she dropped her oar, took the magic paddle from her girdle, and shook it at the *Oni.* She made such funny faces that the *Oni* all burst out laughing.

But the moment they laughed, they could not help throwing up all the water they had drunk, and so the river became full again.

The *Oni* could not cross, so the funny old woman got safely over to the other side and ran away up the road as fast as she could.

She never stopped running until she found herself at home again.

After that she was very happy, for she could make dumplings whenever she pleased. Besides, she had the

The Forty Thieves

In a town in Persia there dwelt two brothers, one named Cassim, the other Ali Baba. Cassim was married to a rich wife and lived in plenty, while Ali Baba had to maintain his wife and children by cutting wood in a neighboring forest and selling it in the town. One day when Ali Baba was in the forest, he saw a troop of men on horseback, coming toward him in a cloud of dust. He was afraid they were robbers and climbed into a tree for safety. When they came up to him and dismounted, he counted forty of them. They unbridled their horses and tied them to trees.

The finest man among them, whom Ali Baba took to be their Captain, went a little way among some bushes and said: "Open, Sesame!" so plainly that Ali Baba heard him. A door opened in the rocks, and, having made the troop go in, he followed them and the door shut again of itself.

They stayed some time inside and Ali Baba, fearing they might come out and catch him, was forced to sit patiently in the tree. At last the door opened again and the Forty Thieves came out. As the Captain went in last he came out first, and made them all pass by him; he then closed the door, saying: "Shut, Sesame!" Every man bridled his horse and mounted; the Captain put himself at their head, and they returned as they came.

Then Ali Baba climbed down and went to the door concealed among the bushes and said: "Open, Sesame!" and it flew open. Ali Baba, who expected a dull, dismal place, was greatly surprised to find it large and well lighted, and hollowed by the hand of man in the form of a vault, which received the light from an opening in the ceiling. He saw rich bales of merchandise — silk stuffs, brocades — all piled together, gold and silver in heaps, and money in leather purses. He went in and the door shut behind him. He did not look at the silver but brought out as many bags of gold as he thought his asses — which were browsing outside — could carry, loaded them with the bags, and hid it all with fagots. Using the words "Shut, Sesame!" he closed the door and went home.

Then he drove his asses into the yard, closed the gates, carried the moneybags to his wife, and emptied them out before her. He bade her keep the secret, and he would bury the gold.

"Let me first measure it," said his wife. "I will borrow a measure from someone, while you dig the hole."

So she ran to the wife of Cassim and borrowed a measure. Knowing Ali Baba's poverty, the sister was curious to find out what sort of grain his wife wished to measure and artfully put some suet at the bottom of the measure. Ali Baba's wife went home and set the measure on the heap of gold and filled it and emptied it often, to her great content. She then carried it back to her sister, without noticing that a piece of gold was sticking to it.

Cassim's wife perceived it directly her back was turned. She grew very curious and said to Cassim when he came home: "Cassim, your brother is richer than you. He does not count his money; he measures it."

He begged her to explain this riddle, which she did by showing him the piece of money and telling him where she found it. Then Cassim grew so envious that he could not sleep and went to his brother in the morning before sunrise.

"Ali Baba," he said, showing him the gold piece: "you pretend to be poor and yet you measure gold."

By this Ali Baba perceived that Cassim and his wife knew his secret, so he confessed all and offered Cassim a share.

"That I expect," said Cassim; "but I must know

where to find the treasure, otherwise I will discover all, and you will lose all.''

Ali Baba, more out of kindness than fear, told him of the cave, and the very words to use. Cassim left Ali Baba, meaning to be beforehand with him and get the treasure for himself. He rose early next morning, and set out with ten mules loaded with great chests. He soon found the place, and the door in the rock. He said: ''Open, Sesame!'' and the door opened and shut behind him.

He could have feasted his eyes all day on the treasure, but he now hastened to gather together as much of it as possible; but when he was ready to go he could not remember what to say for thinking of his great riches. Instead of ''Sesame,'' he said: ''Open, Barley!'' and the door remained fast. He named several different sorts of grain, all but the right one, and the door still stuck fast. He was so frightened at the danger he was in that he had as much forgotten the word as if he had never heard it.

About noon the robbers returned to their cave, and saw Cassim's mules roving about with great chests on their backs. This gave them the alarm. They drew their sabers, and went to the door, which opened on their Captain's saying: ''Open, Sesame!'' Cassim, who had heard the trampling of their horses' feet, resolved to sell his life dearly, so when the door opened he leaped out and threw the Captain down. In vain, however, for the robbers with their sabers soon killed him. On entering the cave they saw all the bags laid ready and could not imagine how anyone had got in without knowing their secret. They cut Cassim's body into four quarters and nailed them up inside the cave, in order to frighten anyone who should venture in, and went away in search of more treasure.

As night drew on, Cassim's wife grew very uneasy and ran to her brother-in-law to tell him where her husband had gone. Ali Baba did his best to comfort her, and set out to the forest in search of Cassim. The first thing he saw on entering the cave was his dead brother. Full of horror, he put the body on one of his asses, and bags of gold on the other two, and, covering all with some fagots, returned home. He drove the two asses laden with gold into his own yard, and led the other to Cassim's house. The door was opened by the slave Morgiana, whom he knew to be both brave and cunning.

Unloading the ass, he said to her: "This is the body of your master, who has been murdered, but whom we must bury as though he had died in his bed. I will speak with you again, but now tell your mistress I have come."

The wife of Cassim, on learning the fate of her husband, broke out into cries and tears, but Ali Baba offered to take her to live with him and his wife if she would promise to keep his counsel and leave everything to Morgiana; whereupon she agreed and dried her eyes.

Morgiana, meanwhile, sought an apothecary and asked him for some lozenges. "My poor master," she said, "can neither eat nor speak, and no one knows what his distemper is." She carried home the lozenges and returned the next day weeping and asked for an essence only given to those just about to die. Thus, in the evening, no one was surprised to hear the shrieks and cries of Cassim's wife and Morgiana, telling everyone that Cassim was dead.

The next day Morgiana went to an old cobbler near the gates of the town, who opened his stall early, put a piece of gold in his hand, and bade him follow her with his needle and thread. Having bound his eyes with a handkerchief, she took him to the room where the body lay, pulled off the bandage, and bade him sew the quarters together. After that she covered his eyes again and led him home.

Then they buried Cassim, and Morgiana, his slave, followed him to the grave, weeping and tearing her hair, while Cassim's wife stayed at home uttering lamentable cries. Next day she went to live with Ali Baba, who gave Cassim's shop to his eldest son.

The Forty Thieves, on their return to the cave, were much astonished to find Cassim's body and some of their moneybags gone.

"We are certainly discovered," said the Captain, "and shall be undone if we cannot find out who it is that knows our secret. Two men must have known it. We have killed one, we must now find the other. To this end one of you who is bold and artful must go into the city dressed as a traveler and discover whom we have killed, and whether men talk of the strange manner of his death. If the messenger fails he must lose his life, lest we be betrayed.''

One of the thieves started up and offered to do this. After the rest had highly commended him for his bravery, he disguised himself, and entered the town at daybreak, just by Baba Mustapha's stall. The thief bade him good day, saying: ''Honest man, how can you possibly see to stitch at your age?''

''Old as I am,'' replied the cobbler, ''I have very good eyes, and you will believe me when I tell you that I sewed a dead body together in a place where I had less light than I have now.''

The robber was overjoyed at his good fortune, and, giving the cobbler a piece of gold, desired to be shown the house where he had stitched up the dead body. At first Mustapha refused, saying that he had been blindfolded; but when the robber gave him another piece of gold, he began to think he might remember the turnings if blindfolded as before. This means succeeded; the robber partly led him, and was partly guided by him, right in front of Cassim's house — the door of which the robber marked with a piece of chalk.

Then, well pleased, he bade farewell to Baba Mustapha and returned to the forest. By and by Morgiana, going out, saw the mark the robber had made, quickly guessed that some mischief was brewing and, fetching a piece of chalk, marked two or three doors on each side, without saying anything to her master or mistress.

The thief, meantime, told his comrades of his discovery. The Captain thanked him and bade him show him the house he had marked. But when they came to it they saw that five or six of the houses were chalked in the same manner. The guide was so confounded that he knew not what answer to make, and when they returned he was at once beheaded for having failed. Another robber was dispatched, and, having won over Baba Mustapha, marked the house in red chalk; but Morgiana being again too clever for them, the second messenger was put to death also.

The Captain now resolved to go himself, but, wiser than the others, he did not mark the house, but looked at it so closely that he could not fail to remember it. He returned and ordered his men to go into the neighboring villages and buy nineteen mules and thirty-eight leather jars, all empty, except one which was full of oil. The captain put one of his men, fully armed, into each, rubbing the outside of the jars with oil from the full vessel. Then the nineteen mules were loaded with thirty-seven robbers in jars, and the jar of oil, and reached the town by dusk.

The Captain stopped his mules in front of Ali Baba's house and said to Ali Baba, who was sitting outside for coolness: "I have brought some oil from a distance to sell at tomorrow's market, but it is now so late that I know not where to pass the night, unless you will do me the favor to take me in.''

Though Ali Baba had seen the Captain of the robbers in the forest, he did not recognize him in the disguise of an oil merchant. He bade him welcome, opened his gates for the mules to enter, and went to Morgiana to bid her prepare a bed and supper for his guest. He brought the stranger into his hall, and after they had supped went again to speak to Morgiana in the kitchen, while the Captain went into the yard under pretense of seeing after his mules, but really to tell his men what to do.

Beginning at the first jar and ending at the last, he said to each man: ''As soon as I throw some stones from the window of the chamber where I lie, cut the jars open with your knives and come out; I will be with you in a trice.''

He returned to the house and Morgiana led him to his chamber. She then told Abdallah, her fellow slave, to set on the pot to make some broth for her master, who had gone to bed. Meanwhile her lamp went out, and she had no more oil in the house.

''Do not be uneasy,'' said Abdallah; ''go into the yard and take some out of one of those jars.''

Morgiana thanked him for his advice, took the oil pot, and went into the yard. When she came to the first jar the robber inside said softly: ''Is it time?''

Any other slave but Morgiana, on finding a man in the jar instead of the oil she wanted, would have screamed and made a noise; but she, knowing the danger her master was in, bethought herself of a plan and answered quietly: "Not yet, but presently."

She went to all the jars, giving the same answer, till she came to the jar of oil. She now saw that her master, thinking to entertain an oil merchant, had let thirty-eight robbers into his house. She filled her oil pot, went back to the kitchen, and, having lit her lamp, went again to the oil jar and filled a large kettle full of oil. When it boiled she poured enough oil into every jar to stifle and kill the robber inside. When this brave deed was done she went back to the kitchen, put out the fire and the lamp, and waited to see what would happen.

In a quarter of an hour the Captain of the robbers awoke, got up, and opened the window. As all seemed quiet he threw down some little pebbles which hit the jars. He listened, and as none of his men seemed to stir, he grew uneasy and went down into the yard. On going to the first jar and saying: "Are you asleep?" he smelt the hot boiled oil and knew at once that his plot to murder Ali Baba and his household had been discovered. He found all the gang were dead and, missing the oil out of the last jar, became aware of the manner of their death. He then forced the lock of a door leading into a garden and climbing over several walls made his escape. Morgiana heard and saw all this and, rejoicing at her success, went to bed and fell asleep.

At daybreak Ali Baba arose and, seeing the oil jars there still, asked why the merchant had not gone with his mules. Morgiana bade him look in the first jar and see if there was any oil. Seeing a man, he started back in terror.

"Have no fear," said Morgiana; "the man cannot harm you. He is dead."

Ali Baba, when he recovered somewhat from his astonishment, asked what had become of the merchant.

"Merchant!" said she. "He is no more a merchant than I am!" And she told him the whole story, assuring him that it was a plot of the robbers of the forest, of whom only three were left, and that the white and red chalk marks had something to do with it. Ali Baba at once gave Morgiana her freedom, saying that he owed her his life. They then buried the bodies in Ali Baba's garden, while the mules were sold in the market by his slaves.

The Captain returned to his lonely cave, which seemed frightful to him without his lost companions, and firmly resolved to avenge them by killing Ali Baba. He dressed himself carefully and went into the town, where he took lodgings at an inn. In the course of a great many journeys to the forest he carried away many rich stuffs and much fine linen, and set up a shop opposite that of Ali Baba's son. He called himself Cogia Hassan, and as he was both civil and well dressed he soon made friends with Ali Baba's son, and through him with Ali Baba, whom he was continually asking to sup with him.

Ali Baba, wishing to return his kindness, invited him

into his house and received him smiling, thanking him
for his kindness to his son. When the merchant was
about to take his leave Ali Baba stopped him, saying:
"Where are you going, sir, in such haste? Will you not
stay and sup with me?"

The merchant refused, saying that he had a reason; on
Ali Baba's asking him what that was, he replied: "It is,
sir, that I can eat no victuals that have any salt in
them."

"If that is all," said Ali Baba, "let me tell you that
there shall be no salt in either the meat or the bread that
we eat tonight."

He went to give this order to Morgiana, who was
much surprised. "Who is this man," she said, "who
eats no salt with his meat?"

"He is an honest man, Morgiana," returned Ali
Baba; "therefore do as I bid you."

But she could not withstand a desire to see this
strange man, so she helped Abdallah carry up the dishes
and saw in a moment that Cogia Hassan was the robber
Captain and carried a dagger under his garment. "I am
not surprised," she said to herself, "that this wicked
man, who intends to kill my master, will eat no salt with
him; but I will hinder his plans."

She sent up the supper by Abdallah, while she made
ready for one of the boldest acts that could be thought
of. When the dessert had been served, Cogia Hassan
was left alone with Ali Baba and his son, both of whom
he thought to make drunk and then murder.

Morgiana, meanwhile, put on a headdress like a dancing-girl's and clasped a girdle round her waist, from which hung a dagger with a silver hilt, and said to Abdallah: "Take your tabor, and let us go and divert our master and his guest."

Abdallah took his tabor and played before Morgiana until they came to the door, where Abdallah stopped playing and Morgiana made a low curtsy.

"Come in, Morgiana," said Ali Baba. "Let Cogia Hassan see what you can do." And turning to his guest, he said: "She is my housekeeper."

Cogia Hassan was by no means pleased, for he feared that his chance of killing Ali Baba was gone for the present; but he pretended great eagerness to see Morgiana, and Abdallah began to play and Morgiana to dance. After she had performed several dances she drew her dagger and made passes with it, sometimes pointing it at her own breast, sometimes at her master's, as if it were part of the dance. Suddenly, out of breath, she snatched the tabor from Abdallah with her left hand, and, holding the dagger in her right, held out the tabor to her master. Ali Baba and his son put a piece of gold into it, and Cogia Hassan, seeing that she was coming to him, pulled out his purse to make her a present, but while he was putting his hand into it Morgiana plunged the dagger into his heart.

"Unhappy girl!" cried Ali Baba and his son. "What have you done to ruin us?"

"It was to preserve you, master, not to ruin you,"

answered Morgiana. "See here," she cried, opening the false merchant's garment and showing the dagger; "see what an enemy you have entertained! Remember, he would eat no salt with you, and what more would you have? Look at him! He is both the false oil merchant and the Captain of the Forty Thieves."

Ali Baba was so grateful to Morgiana for thus saving his life that he offered her in marriage to his son, who readily consented; and a few days after the wedding was celebrated with great splendor. At the end of a year Ali Baba, hearing nothing of the two remaining robbers, judged they were dead and set out to the cave. The door opened on his saying: "Open, Sesame!" He went in and saw that nobody had been there since the Captain left it. He brought away as much gold as he could carry and returned to town. He told his son the secret of the cave, which his son handed down in his turn, so the children and grandchildren of Ali Baba were rich to the end of their lives.

Andrew Lang

Kate Crackernuts

Once upon a time there was a king and a queen, as in many lands there have been. The king had a daughter, Anne, and the queen had one named Kate; but Anne was far bonnier than the queen's daughter, though they loved one another like real sisters. The queen was jealous of the king's daughter being bonnier than her own and cast about to spoil her beauty. So she took counsel of the henwife, who told her to send the lassie to her next morning, fasting.

So next morning early, the queen said to Anne, "Go, my dear, to the henwife in the glen and ask her for some eggs." So Anne set out; but as she passed through the kitchen she saw a crust, and she took and munched it as she went along.

When she came to the henwife's, she asked for eggs, as she had been told to do; and the henwife said to her, "Lift the lid off that pot there and see." The lassie did so, but nothing happened. "Go home to your minnie and tell her to keep her larder door better locked," said the henwife. So she went home to the queen and told her what the henwife had said. The queen knew from this that the lassie had had something to eat, so she watched the next morning and sent her away fasting; but the princess saw some countryfolk picking peas by the roadside, and being very kind, she spoke to them and took a handful of the peas, which she ate by the way.

When she came to the henwife's, the henwife said, "Lift the lid off the pot and you'll see." So Anne lifted the lid but nothing happened. Then the henwife was rare angry and said to Anne, "Tell your minnie the pot won't boil if the fire's away." So Anne went home and told the queen.

The third day the queen went along with the girl herself to the henwife. Now, this time, when Anne lifted the lid off the pot, off fell her own pretty head, and on jumped a sheep's head.

So the queen was now quite satisfied and went back home.

Her own daughter, Kate, however, took a fine linen cloth and wrapped it round her sister's head and took her by the hand as they both went out to seek their fortune. They went on, and they went on, and they went on, till they came to a castle. Kate knocked at the door and asked for a night's lodging for herself and a sick sister. They went in and found it was a king's castle, who had two sons. One of them was sickening away to death, and no one could find out what ailed him. And the curious thing was that whoever watched him at night was never seen anymore. So the king offered a peck of silver to anyone who would stay up with him. Now Katie was a very brave girl, so she offered to sit up with him.

Till midnight all went well. As twelve o'clock rang, however, the sick prince rose, dressed himself, and slipped downstairs. Kate followed, but he didn't seem to notice her. The prince went to the stable, saddled his horse, called his hound, and jumped into the saddle, and Kate leapt lightly up behind him. Away they rode through the greenwood with Kate, as they passed, plucking nuts from the trees and filling her apron with them. They rode on and on till they came to a green hill. The prince drew bridle here and spoke: "Open, open, green hill, and let the young prince in with his horse and his hound"; and Kate added, "and his lady behind him."

Immediately the green hill opened and they passed in. The prince entered a magnificent hall, brightly lighted up, and many beautiful fairies surrounded the prince and led him off to the dance. Meanwhile, Kate, without being noticed, hid herself behind the door. There she saw the prince dancing and dancing and dancing, till he could dance no longer and fell upon a couch. Then the fairies fanned him till he could rise again and go on dancing.

At last the cock crowed, and the prince made all haste to get on horseback; Kate jumped up behind and home they rode. When the morning sun rose, the folk came in and found Kate sitting down by the fire, cracking her nuts. Kate said the prince had had a good night, but she would not sit up another night unless she was to get a peck of gold. The second night passed as the first had. The prince got up at midnight and rode away to the green hill and the fairy ball; and Kate went with him, gathering nuts as they rode through the forest. This time she did not watch the prince, for she knew he would dance and dance and dance. But she saw a fairy baby playing with a wand and overheard one of the fairies say: "Three strokes of that wand would make Kate's sick sister as bonnie as ever she was." So Kate rolled nuts to the fairy baby till the baby toddled after the nuts and let fall the wand, which Kate took up and put in her apron. At cockcrow they rode home as before. The moment Kate got home to her room she rushed to touch Anne three times with the wand; the nasty sheep's head fell off, and she was her own pretty self again. The third night Kate consented to watch only if she should marry the sick prince. All went on as on the first two nights. This time the fairy baby was playing with a birdie, and Kate heard one of the fairies say: "Three bites of that birdie would make the sick prince as well as ever he was." Kate rolled all the nuts

she had to the fairy baby till the birdie was dropped, and Kate put it in her apron.

At cockcrow they set off again, but instead of cracking her nuts as she used to do, this time Kate plucked the feathers off and cooked the birdie. Soon there arose a very savory smell. "Oh!" said the sick prince, "I wish I had a bite of that birdie," so Kate gave him a bite of the birdie, and he rose up on his elbow. By and by he cried out again: "Oh, if I had another bite of that birdie!" So Kate gave him another bite, and he sat up on his bed. Then he said again: "Oh! If I but had a third bite of the birdie!" So Kate gave him a third bite, and he rose hale and strong, dressed himself, and sat down by the fire; and when the folk came in next morning they found Kate and the young prince cracking nuts together. Meanwhile his brother had seen Annie and had fallen in love with her, as everybody did who saw her sweet pretty face. So the sick son married the well sister, and the well son married the sick sister; and they all lived happy and died happy, and never drank out of a dry cappie.

Joseph Jacobs

Clever Grethel

There was once a cook, and her name was Grethel. She wore shoes with red rosettes on them, and when she went walking in these shoes she would turn herself this way and that, saying: "Well I never, you *are* a handsome creature!"

At night as she combed her hair in the glass she would say: "My! So there you are!" And they called her "clever Grethel."

Whenever after a walk she came home to her master's house again, she would always take a little sippet of wine. "You see, Grethel, my dear, it makes the tongue able to *taste* better," she would say. "And what's a cook without a tongue?" In fact, Grethel kept her tongue very busy, nibbling and tasting.

Now one day her master said to her: "I have a guest coming this evening, Grethel, and a guest that knows what's what, and I want you to roast us a pair of fowls for supper. Two, mind you, young and tender. And I want 'em roasted to a turn."

Grethel said: "Why, yes, master. They shall taste so good you won't know what you're eating."

So she killed two fowls, scalded and plucked them, tucked in their legs with a little bit of liver in between, stuffed them with stuffing, and towards evening put them down to a clear, red fire to roast. She basted and basted them, and when they were done to a turn and smelt sweet as Arabia, and their breasts were a rich, clear, delicate brown, Grethel called out to her master:

"If that guest of yours don't come soon, master, I shall have to take the fowls away from the fire. And I warn you, they will be utterly spoilt, for they are just at their juiciest."

Her master said: "So, so! I will run out and see if he is coming."

As soon as her master had turned his back, Grethel thought to herself she would have another sip of something to drink. Having had one sip, she took another sip, and then another. Then she basted the fowls again, and twisted the spit. She puffed with the heat, the fire blazing in her face. Suddenly, as she stood looking at the fowls, she thought to herself: "Now cooking's cooking! I shouldn't wonder if them birds taste as good as they smell. Oh, oh, oh! It's a sin. It's a shame!"

Then she looked out of the window; and when she saw that nobody was coming, she said to herself: "There! What did I tell you? And lawks! one of the wings is burning." So she cut off the wing with a twist of her sharp knife, and holding it between her finger and thumb, ate every scrap of it up, to the very bone.

Then, "Dear me," she sighed to herself, looking at the chicken, "that one wing left looks like another wing missing!" So she ate up the other. Then she took another sip of wine, and once more looked at the fowls.

"Now think what a sad thing," she said. "Once those two poor hens were sisters, and you couldn't tell 'em apart. But now look at them: one whole and the other nowt but legs!" So she gobbled up the wings of the other chicken to make the pair look more alike. And still her master did not come. Then said she to herself:

"Lor', Grethel, my dear, why worry? There won't be any guest to-night. He has forgotten all about it. And master can have some nice dry bread and cheese." With that she ate up completely one of the chickens, skin, stuffing, gravy and all, and then, seeing how sad and lonely the other looked all by itself with its legs sticking up in the air and both its wings gone, she finished off that too.

She was picking the very last sweet morsel off its wishbone when her master came running into the kitchen, and cried: "Quick, Grethel! Dish up! Dish up! Our guest has just turned the corner."

At this moment she was standing in front of the fire in

her fine shoes and great cooking apron, and she looked over her shoulder at her master. But he at once rushed out to see if the table was ready, and the wine on it, snatched up the great carving-knife, and began to sharpen it on the doorstep.

Pretty soon after, the guest came to the door and knocked. Grethel ran softly out, caught him by the sleeve, pushed him out of the porch, pressed her finger on her lips, and whispered: "Ssh! Ssh! On your life! Listen, now, and be off, I beseech you! My poor master has gone clean out of his senses at your being so late. Mad! Mad! If he catches you, he will cut your ears off. Hark now! He is sharpening his knife on the doorstep!"

At this the guest turned pale as ashes, and hearing the steady rasping of the knife on the stone, ran off down the street as fast as his legs could carry him. As soon as he was out of sight, Grethel hastened back to her master.

"La, master!" she said, *"you've* asked a nice fine guest to supper!"

"Why," says he, looking up with the knife in his hand, "what's wrong with him?"

"Wrong!" says she. "Why, he had scarce put his nose in at the door, when he gives a sniff. 'What! Chicken!' says he, 'roast chicken!' And away he rushed into the kitchen, snatched up my two poor beeootiful birds, and without even waiting for the dish or the gravy, ran off with them down the street."

"What, *now*?" said her master.

"This very minute!" said Grethel.

"Both?" said her master.

"Both," said she.

"Heaven save us!" said her master. "Then I shall have nothing for supper!" And off he ran in chase of his guest, as fast as he could pelt, crying out as he did so:

"Hi, there! Stop! Stop! Hi! Just one! Just one! Only one!"

But the guest, hearing these words, and supposing that the madman behind him with his long knife meant one of his ears, ran on faster than ever into the darkness of the night.

And Grethel sat down, happy and satisfied. She gave one deep sigh, looked solemnly at the two bright red rosettes on her shoes, and had another sip or two of wine.

Walter de la Mare

Cap o' Rushes

Well, there was once a very rich gentleman, who had three daughters, and he thought he'd see how fond they were of him. So he says to the first, "How much do you love me, my dear?"

"Why," says she, "as I love my life."

"That's good," says he.

So he says to the second, "How much do *you* love me, my dear?"

"Why," says she, "better nor all the world."

"That's good," says he.

So he says to the third, "How much do *you* love me, my dear?"

"Why, I love you as fresh meat loves salt," says she.

Well, but he was angry. "You don't love me at all,"

says he, "and in my house you stay no more." So he drove her out there and then, and shut the door in her face.

Well, she went away and on and on till she came to a fen. There she gathered a lot of rushes and made them into a kind of a cloak with a hood, to cover her from head to foot and to hide her fine clothes. Then she went on and on till she came to a great house.

"Do you want a maid?" says she.

"No, we don't," said they.

"I haven't nowhere to go," says she; "and I ask no wages and do any sort of work."

"Well," said they, "if you would like to wash the pots and scrape the saucepans you may stay."

So she stayed there and washed the pots and scraped the saucepans and did all the dirty work. And because she gave no name they called her "Cap o' Rushes."

Well, one day there was to be a great dance a little way off, and the servants were allowed to go and look on at the grand people. Cap o' Rushes said she was too tired to go, so she stayed at home.

But when they were gone, she offed with her cap o' rushes, cleaned herself, and went to the dance. And no one there was so finely dressed as she.

Well, who should be there but her master's son, and what should he do but fall in love with her the minute he set eyes on her. He wouldn't dance with anyone else.

But before the dance was done, Cap o' Rushes slipped off, and away she went home. And when the other maids came back, she was pretending to be asleep with her cap o' rushes on.

Well, next morning they said to her, "You did miss a sight, Cap o' Rushes!"

"What was that?" says she.

"Why, the beautifullest lady you ever see, dressed gay and ga'. The young master, he never took his eyes off her."

"Well, I should have liked to have seen her," says Cap o' Rushes.

"Well, there's to be another dance this evening, and perhaps she'll be there."

But, come the evening, Cap o' Rushes said she was too tired to go with them. However, when they were gone, she offed with her cap o' rushes, cleaned herself, and away she went to the dance.

The master's son had been reckoning on seeing her, and he danced with no one else and never took his eyes off her. But, before the dance was over, she slipped off, and home she went. And when the maids came back she pretended to be asleep with her cap o' rushes on.

Next day they said to her again, "Well, Cap o' Rushes, you should ha' been there to see the lady. There she was again, gay and ga', and the young master he never took his eyes off her."

"Well, there," says she, "I should ha' liked to ha' seen her."

"Well," says they, "there's a dance again this evening, and you must go with us, for she's sure to be there.''

Well, come this evening, Cap o' Rushes said she was too tired to go, and do what they would she stayed at home. But when they were gone she offed with her cap o' rushes, cleaned herself, and away she went to the dance.

The master's son was rarely glad when he saw her. He danced with none but her and never took his eyes off her. When she wouldn't tell him her name, nor where she came from, he gave her a ring and told her if he didn't see her again he should die.

Well, before the dance was over, off she slipped, and home she went. And when the maids came home she was pretending to be asleep with her cap o' rushes on.

Well, next day they said to her, ''There, Cap o' Rushes, you didn't come last night, and now you won't see the lady, for there's no more dances.''

''Well, I should have rarely liked to have seen her,'' says she.

The master's son he tried every way to find out where the lady was gone, but go where he might, and ask whom he might, he never heard anything about her. And he got worse and worse for the love of her till he had to keep to his bed.

''Make some gruel for the young master,'' they said to the cook. ''He's dying for the love of the lady.'' The cook set about making it, when Cap o' Rushes came in.

"What are you a-doing of?" says she.

"I'm going to make some gruel for the young master," says the cook, "for he's dying for love of the lady."

"Let me make it," says Cap o' Rushes.

Well, the cook wouldn't at first, but at last she said yes, and Cap o' Rushes made the gruel. And when she had made it, she slipped the ring into it on the sly before the cook took it upstairs.

The young man he drank it, and then he saw the ring at the bottom.

"Send for the cook," says he.

So up she comes.

"Who made this gruel here?" says he.

"I did," says the cook, for she was frightened.

And he looked at her.

"No, you didn't," says he. "Say who did it, and you shan't be harmed."

"Well, then, 'twas Cap o' Rushes," says she.

"Send Cap o' Rushes here," says he.

So Cap o' Rushes came.

"Did you make my gruel?" says he.

"Yes, I did," says she.

"Where did you get this ring?" says he.

"From him that gave it me," says she.

"Who are you, then?" says the young man.

"I'll show you," says she. And she offed with her cap o' rushes, and there she was in her beautiful clothes.

Well, the master's son he got well very soon, and

they were to be married in a little time. It was to be a very grand wedding, and everyone was asked far and near. And Cap o' Rushes's father was asked. But she never told anybody who she was.

But before the wedding, she went to the cook, and says she: "I want you to dress every dish without a mite of salt."

"That'll be rare nasty," says the cook.

"That doesn't signify," says she.

"Very well," says the cook.

Well, the wedding day came, and they were married. And after they were married, all the company sat down to the dinner. When they began to eat the meat, it was so tasteless they couldn't eat it. But Cap o' Rushes's father tried first one dish and then another, and then he burst out crying.

"What is the matter?" said the master's son to him.

"Oh!" says he, "I had a daughter. And I asked her how much she loved me. And she said, 'As much as fresh meat loves salt.' And I turned her from my door, for I thought she didn't love me. And now I see she loved me best of all. And she may be dead for ought I know."

"No, father, here she is!" said Cap o' Rushes. And she went to him and put her arms round him.

And so they were all happy ever after.

Joseph Jacobs

The Lass Who Went Out at the Cry of Dawn

There was once a lass who went out at the cry of dawn to wash her face in the morning dew to make it bonnier, and she never came home again.

Her father searched for her, and her mother wept for her, but all her father's searching and her mother's grieving didn't fetch the lass back home.

She had a younger sister who loved her dearly, and who said she'd go herself into the wide world and travel about to find her sister and she'd not come home till she found her, for she wasn't content to bide at home without her.

So her father gave the younger sister his blessing to take along with her, and a purse with a piece of gold in it to help her on her way.

Her mother made up a packet of things for her to take along. There was a bobbin of yarn and a golden needle, a paper of pins and a silver thimble, and a wee sharp knife all done up in a fair white towel. And she had her mother's blessing, too.

She wandered up and down the world for many a weary day. Then in her wanderings, some one told her there was a wicked wizard who lived on Mischanter Hill who was known to steal young maids away, and maybe 'twas he who had taken the lass's older sister.

Now that the lass knew where she was going, she wandered no more, but off she made for Mischanter Hill.

When she got there, she saw 'twould be a terrible hard climb, for the road was steep and rocky all the way. So she sat down on a stone at the foot to rest a bit before she went on.

While she was sitting there, along came a tinker body. He was between the shafts of a cart loaded with pots and kettles and pans, lugging it and tugging it along the stony road. He stopped when he saw the younger sister and gave her a "good day."

"Lawks!" said she to him. " 'Tis a wearisome task to be doing the work of a horse."

" 'Tis that!" the tinker agreed, "but beggars cannot be choosers. I've no money to buy a horse so I must just go on moiling and toiling with my load."

"Well now," said she, "I've a bit of gold my father gave me I've ne'er had need for. 'Tis doing nobody any good while it lies in my pocket. Take it and welcome, and buy yourself a horse.''

The tinker took the purse in his hand and looked at her. "I've been pulling that load for a weary long time," said he, "and though I've met many on my way, not one has given me as much as a kind word before. If you are going up the hill to the wizard's castle, I'll give you a few words to take along with you. What you see and what you hear are not what they seem to be. And my advice to you is that you'd better far go back the way you came, for the wizard who lives at the top of the hill will enchant you if he can. But I doubt you'll heed it.''

"That I won't," said the lass. "But thank you kindly, anyway.'' So the tinker turned his cart about and went back down the road while the lass began to climb the long steep hill.

When she got about halfway up the hill, she came across a poor ragged bodach standing by the road. His clothes were all tatters and patches, and he was pinning the rents together with thorns. As fast as he pinned them, the thorns broke, so he'd have to start all over again.

"Lawks," said the lass. " 'Tis wearisome work trying to mend with thorns. Now, hold a bit," said she. "I've a paper of pins my mother gave me that I've ne'er had use for. They're no good to anybody while they lie in my bundle. Take them and do your mending with them.''

The poor ragged bodach took the pins and he looked at her and said, "I've stood here many a weary day, and many have passed me by, but no one ever gave me so much as a kind word before. I've naught to give in return but a few words for you to take along with you. Gold and silver are a match for evil. If you're going up to the wizard's castle, my advice to you is to turn back and go the way you came, because he's a terribly wicked wizard and he'll lay a spell upon you if he can. But I doubt you'll take it."

"That I won't!" said she. "But thank you kindly, anyway."

So she left the poor bodach there, mending his clothes with the pins, and went on up to the top of the hill.

When she got to the top of the hill, there was the wizard's castle standing across a big courtyard inside a high stone wall. She opened the gates, and went across the courtyard, and knocked boldly on the castle door. The wizard himself opened it to her. The minute she saw him she knew who he was for there was such evil in his face as she'd never seen before. But he spoke to her politely enough and asked her what she'd come for.

"I'd like my older sister," said she, "for I hear you've brought her here."

"Come in," said he, throwing the door wide. "I'll see if I can find her." He took her into a room and left her there, and shut the door behind him.

She looked about the room, but there was no sign of her sister anywhere, so she sat down to wait. All of a sudden she heard flames crackling, and the room was filled with smoke. The flames sprang at her from the walls, and she could feel their heat. "Lawks!" she cried. "The castle's on fire!" And she was about to spring from her chair and run away from the room when she remembered what the tinker body had said: What you see and hear are not what they seem to be! Then said she, "Och, no doubt 'tis only some of the wizard's magic arts." So she paid the smoke and the flames no heed, and they went away.

She sat back in the chair and waited again for a while, and then she heard a voice calling and weeping. It was the voice of her sister that she was seeking, and she was calling her by name. The lass jumped from her chair, ready to run and find her sister. Then she remembered the tinker's words again: What you see and hear are not what they seem to be. Said she, "Och, 'tis only the wizard's magic again, to be sure." But the voice went on calling her, and she could scarce keep her feet from running to find where it came from. So she took the bobbin of yarn from her packet and bound her arm to the chair, passing the yarn round and round until it was all used up. Now she was safe, for no matter how she pulled, the yarn held fast. After a while the voice stopped calling, and the sound of the weeping died away and all was still. Then the lass took out the wee knife and cut herself free from the chair.

Just after that, the wizard came back and when he saw her sitting there, waiting, he looked surprised and

not too pleased. But he told her to come along with him and maybe they'd find her sister. There were a lot of maidens came from here and there to the castle, he told her. She'd have to pick her sister out for herself.

They went along to another room and when she went in she stopped and stared. There was nothing at all in the room but seven white statues. Every one of them was as white as snow from head to foot, and they were as like each other as seven peas, and every one was the image of her sister.

"Pick your sister out," said the wizard with a terribly wicked grin. "You may take her along with you and welcome!" said he. He thought she'd never be able to do it.

The lass walked up and down before the statues. She couldn't for the life of her tell which one she ought to be choosing. So at last she stood still, with her chin in her hand, considering what to do next. Then she remembered the words the ragged bodach had given her in return for the paper of pins. Gold and silver are a match for evil! So she took the silver thimble out of her pocket and slipped it on the finger of the first statue. She'd no sooner done so than the thimble turned black as a coal. That wasn't her sister at all! So she tried it on the rest of the statues one by one, and the thimble stayed black as black could ever be, until it came to the last one in the line. She put the thimble on that one's finger, and the thimble shone out so bright it fair dazzled her eyes. "I'll just take this one!" she told the wizard. As she spoke the statue moved, and there was her sister turned back to flesh and blood, with her own rosy cheeks and golden hair and clear blue eyes.

The younger sister took her older sister's hand and the two of them went out of the room and down the hall, and through the door of the castle.

When the wizard saw they were getting away from him, he nearly burst with the furious rage he had in him. With his magic arts he called up a great fierce wolf and sent it after them. The two sisters heard it come panting along behind them and they took to their heels. They ran like the wind itself, but the wolf came closer and closer. The older sister wept and said she could run no more. But the ragged bodach's words came into the mind of the younger sister. She cried out, "Gold and silver are a match for evil!"

Quick as a wink she whipped the golden needle out of her packet, and turned to face the wolf. He came snapping and snarling up to her with his jaws wide open, ready to leap at her. She reached out and thrust the needle straightway betwixt his great red eyes. That was the end of the wolf, for he dinged down dead.

The wizard shrieked with rage, and came flying at them himself with his black cloak outspread, bearing him through the air like a pair of wings. All the lass had left was the wee sharp knife, and no words of the tinker body and the old bodach left to tell her what to do. But since the knife was all she had, she'd have to make do with it and hope for the best. She put her hand in the packet to pull it out, and somehow the knife got tangled up with her mother's and father's blessings. So when the wizard got close enough, and she aimed the knife at him, the blessings carried it straight to his heart and down he fell, black cloak and all!

Whilst they stood there getting their breath, they heard a great rumbling noise. They looked over at the castle, and it was rocking to and fro before their eyes. All of a sudden it turned to dust and settled down in a heap on the ground. Being made of the wizard's magic, it could no longer stand, now that the wizard was dead.

The two sisters had no need to run anymore. They walked down the mountain as if they were walking on the clouds of the air, instead of the rocky steep road.

Halfway down they met up with a fine young man all dressed in the best of clothes. "You'll not be remembering me, I doubt," said he to the younger sister. "I'm the ragged bodach you gave your paper of pins to. The wizard laid a spell on me that I'd be mending my clothes with thorns till the end of time. But now the spell is lifted, and I'm a free man once more."

The younger sister would never have known him, had it not been that she saw his clothes were all stuck through with pins.

The three of them walked down the hill together, and what should they find there but a fine young man standing beside a grand shining coach. "You'll not be remembering me," said he. "I'm the tinker body that you gave your purse with the gold piece in it to."

She'd ne'er have known him had he not taken the purse from his pocket and given it back. The wizard had laid a spell on him, too, but now that the wizard was dead, the spell was lifted and he was free.

The four of them got into the coach and drove back home. So the younger sister brought her older sister back with her, just as she'd said she would. The older sister married the fine young man with the pins, and the younger sister married the tinker body, and they all settled down together happily all the rest of their days.

Sorche Nic Leodhas

Three Strong Women (A Tall Tale From Japan)

Long ago, in Japan, there lived a famous wrestler, and he was on his way to the capital city to wrestle before the Emperor.

He strode down the road on legs thick as the trunks of small trees. He had been walking for seven hours and could, and probably would, walk for seven more without getting tired.

The time was autumn, the sky was a cold, watery blue, the air chilly. In the small bright sun, the trees along the roadside glowed red and orange.

The wrestler hummed to himself, "Zun-zun-zun," in time with the long swing of his legs. Wind blew through his thin brown robe, and he wore no sword at his side. He felt proud that he needed no sword, even in the darkest and loneliest places. The icy air on his body only reminded him that few tailors would have been able to make expensive warm clothes for a man so broad and tall. He felt much as a wrestler should — strong, healthy, and rather conceited.

A soft roar of fast-moving water beyond the trees told him that he was passing above a river bank. He "zun-zunned" louder; he loved the sound of his voice and wanted it to sound clearly above the rushing water.

He thought: They call me Forever-Mountain because I am such a good strong wrestler — big, too. I'm a fine, brave man and far too modest ever to say so . . .

Just then he saw a girl who must have come up from the river, for she steadied a bucket on her head.

Her hands on the bucket were small, and there was a dimple on each thumb, just below the knuckle. She was a round little girl with red cheeks and a nose like a friendly button. Her eyes looked as though she were thinking of ten thousand funny stories at once. She clambered up onto the road and walked ahead of the wrestler, jolly and bounceful.

"If I don't tickle that fat girl, I shall regret it all my life," said the wrestler under his breath. "She's sure to go 'squeak' and I shall laugh and laugh. If she drops her bucket, that will be even funnier — and I can always run and fill it again and even carry it home for her."

He tiptoed up and poked her lightly in the ribs with one huge finger.

"Kochokochokocho!" he said, a fine, ticklish sound in Japanese.

The girl gave a satisfying squeal, giggled, and brought one arm down so that the wrestler's hand was caught between it and her body.

"Ho-ho-ho! You've caught me! I can't move at all!" said the wrestler, laughing.

"I know," said the jolly girl.

He felt that it was very good-tempered of her to take a joke so well, and started to pull his hand free.

Somehow, he could not.

He tried again, using a little more strength.

"Now, now — let me go, little girl," he said. "I am a very powerful man. If I pull too hard I might hurt you."

"Pull," said the girl. "I admire powerful men."

She began to walk, and though the wrestler tugged and pulled until his feet dug great furrows in the ground, he had to follow. She couldn't have paid him less attention if he had been a puppy — a small one.

Ten minutes later, still tugging while trudging helplessly after her, he was glad that the road was lonely and no one was there to see.

"Please let me go," he pleaded. "I am the famous wrestler Forever-Mountain. I must go and show my strength before the Emperor" — he burst out weeping from shame and confusion — "and you're hurting my hand!"

The girl steadied the bucket on her head with her free

hand and dimpled sympathetically over her shoulder. "You poor, sweet little Forever-Mountain," she said. "Are you tired? Shall I carry you? I can leave the water here and come back for it later."

"I do not want you to carry me. I want you to let me go, and then I want to forget I ever saw you. What do you want with me?" moaned the pitiful wrestler.

"I only want to help you," said the girl, now pulling him steadily up and up a narrow mountain path. "Oh, I am sure you'll have no more trouble than anyone else when you come up against the other wrestlers. You'll win, or else you'll lose, and you won't be too badly hurt either way. But aren't you afraid you might meet a really *strong* man someday?"

Forever-Mountain turned white. He stumbled. He was imagining being laughed at throughout Japan as "Hardly-Ever-Mountain."

She glanced back.

"You see? Tired already," she said. "I'll walk more slowly. Why don't you come along to my mother's house and let us make a strong man of you? The wrestling in the capital isn't due to begin for three months. I know, because Grandmother thought she'd go. You'd be spending all that time in bad company and wasting what little power you have."

"All right. Three months. I'll come along," said the wrestler. He felt he had nothing more to lose. Also, he feared that the girl might become angry if he refused, and place him in the top of a tree until he changed his mind.

"Fine," she said happily. "We are almost there."

She freed his hand. It had become red and a little swollen. "But if you break your promise and run off, I shall have to chase you and carry you back."

Soon they arrived in a small valley. A simple farmhouse with a thatched roof stood in the middle.

"Grandmother is at home, but she is an old lady and she's probably sleeping." The girl shaded her eyes with one hand. "But Mother should be bringing our cow back from the field — oh, there's Mother now!"

She waved. The woman coming around the corner of the house put down the cow she was carrying and waved back.

She smiled and came across the grass, walking with a lively bounce like her daughter's. Well, maybe her bounce was a little more solid, thought the wrestler.

"Excuse me," she said, brushing some cow hair from her dress and dimpling, also like her daughter. "These mountain paths are full of stones. They hurt the cow's feet. And who is the nice young man you've brought, Maru-me?"

The girl explained. "And we have only three months!" she finished anxiously.

"Well, it's not long enough to do much, but it's not so short a time that we can't do something," said her mother, looking thoughtful. "But he does look terribly feeble. He'll need a lot of good things to eat. Maybe when he gets stronger he can help Grandmother with some of the easy work about the house.''

''That will be fine!'' said the girl, and she called her grandmother — loudly, for the old lady was a little deaf.

''I'm coming!'' came a creaky voice from inside the house, and a little old woman leaning on a stick and looking very sleepy tottered out of the door. As she came toward them she stumbled over the roots of a great oak tree.

''Heh! My eyes aren't what they used to be. That's the fourth time this month I've stumbled over that tree,'' she complained and, wrapping her skinny arms about its trunk, pulled it out of the ground.

''Oh, Grandmother! You should have let me pull it up for you,'' said Maru-me.

''Hm. I hope I didn't hurt my poor old back,'' muttered the old lady. She called out, ''Daughter! Throw that tree away like a good girl, so no one will fall over it. But make sure it doesn't hit anybody.''

''You can help Mother with the tree,'' Maru-me said to Forever-Mountain. ''On second thought, you'd better not help. Just watch.''

Her mother went to the tree, picked it up in her two hands, and threw it — clumsily and with a little gasp, the way a woman throws. Up went the tree, sailing end over end, growing smaller and smaller as it flew. It landed with a faint crash far up the mountainside.

"Ah, how clumsy," she said. "I meant to throw it *over* the mountain. It's probably blocking the path now, and I'll have to get up early tomorrow to move it."

The wrestler was not listening. He had very quietly fainted.

"Oh! We must put him to bed," said Maru-me.

"Poor, feeble young man," said her mother.

"I hope we can do something for him. Here, let me carry him, he's light," said the grandmother. She slung him over her shoulder and carried him into the house, creaking along with her cane.

The next day they began the work of making Forever-Mountain over into what they thought a strong man should be. They gave him the simplest food to eat, and the toughest. Day by day they prepared his rice with less and less water, until no ordinary man could have chewed or digested it.

Every day he was made to do the work of five men, and every evening he wrestled with Grandmother. Maru-me and her mother agreed that Grandmother, being old and feeble, was the least likely to injure him accidentally. They hoped the exercise might be good for the old lady's rheumatism.

He grew stronger and stronger but was hardly aware of it. Grandmother could still throw him easily into the air — and catch him again — without ever changing her sweet old smile.

He quite forgot that outside this valley he was one of the greatest wrestlers in Japan and was called Forever-Mountain. His legs had been like logs; now they were like pillars. His big hands were hard as stones, and when he cracked his knuckles the sound was like trees splitting on a cold night.

Sometimes he did an exercise that wrestlers do in Japan — raising one foot high above the ground and bringing it down with a crash. Then people in nearby villages looked up at the winter sky and told one another that it was very late in the year for thunder.

Soon he could pull up a tree as well as the grandmother. He could even throw one — but only a small distance. One evening, near the end of his third month, he wrestled with Grandmother and held her down for half a minute.

"Heh-heh!" She chortled and got up, smiling with every wrinkle. "I would never have believed it!"

Maru-me squealed with joy and threw her arms around him — gently, for she was afraid of cracking his ribs.

"Very good, very good! What a strong man," said her mother, who had just come home from the fields, carrying, as usual, the cow. She put the cow down and patted the wrestler on the back.

They agreed that he was now ready to show some *real* strength before the Emperor.

"Take the cow along with you tomorrow when you go," said the mother. "Sell her and buy yourself a belt — a silken belt. Buy the fattest and heaviest one you can find. Wear it when you appear before the Emperor, as a souvenir from us.''

"I wouldn't think of taking your only cow. You've already done too much for me. And you'll need her to plow the fields, won't you?"

They burst out laughing, Maru-me squealed, her mother roared. The grandmother cackled so hard and long that she choked and had to be pounded on the back.

"Oh, dear," said the mother, still laughing. "You didn't think we used our cow for anything like *work!* Why, Grandmother here is stronger than five cows!"

"The cow is our pet." Maru-me giggled. "She has lovely brown eyes."

"But it really gets tiresome having to carry her back and forth each day so that she has enough grass to eat," said her mother.

"Then you must let me give you all the prize money that I win," said Forever-Mountain.

"Oh, no! We wouldn't think of it!" said Maru-me. "Because we all like you too much to sell you anything. And it is not proper to accept gifts of money from strangers."

"True," said Forever-Mountain. "I will now ask your mother's and grandmother's permission to marry you. I want to be one of the family."

"Oh! I'll get a wedding dress ready!" said Maru-me.

The mother and grandmother pretended to consider very seriously, but they quickly agreed.

Next morning Forever-Mountain tied his hair up in the topknot that all Japanese wrestlers wear, and got ready to leave. He thanked Maru-me and her mother and bowed very low to the grandmother, since she was the oldest and had been a fine wrestling partner.

Then he picked up the cow in his arms and trudged up the mountain. When he reached the top, he slung the cow over one shoulder and waved good-by to Maru-me.

At the first town he came to, Forever-Mountain sold the cow. She brought a good price because she was unusually fat from never having worked in her life. With the money, he bought the heaviest silken belt he could find.

When he reached the palace grounds, many of the other wrestlers were already there, sitting about, eating enormous bowls of rice, comparing one another's weight and telling stories. They paid little attention to Forever-Mountain, except to wonder why he had arrived so late this year. Some of them noticed that he had grown very quiet and took no part at all in their boasting.

All the ladies and gentlemen of the court were waiting in a special courtyard for the wrestling to begin. They wore many robes, one on top of another, heavy with embroidery and gold cloth, and sweat ran down their faces and froze in the winter afternoon. The gentlemen had long swords so weighted with gold and precious stones that they could never have used them, even if they had known how. The court ladies, with their long black hair hanging down behind, had their faces painted dead white, which made them look frightened. They had pulled out their real eyebrows and painted new ones high above the place where eyebrows are supposed to be, and this made them all look as though they were very surprised at something.

Behind a screen sat the Emperor — by himself, because he was too noble for ordinary people to look at. He was a lonely old man with a kind, tired face. He hoped the wrestling would end quickly so that he could go to his room and write poems.

The first two wrestlers chosen to fight were Forever-Mountain and a wrestler who was said to have the biggest stomach in the country. He and Forever-Mountain both threw some salt into the ring. It was understood that this drove away evil spirits.

Then the other wrestler, moving his stomach somewhat out of the way, raised his foot and brought it down with a fearful stamp. He glared fiercely at Forever-Mountain as if to say, "Now *you* stamp, you poor frightened man!"

Forever-Mountain raised his foot. He brought it down.

There was a sound like thunder, the earth shook, and the other wrestler bounced into the air and out of the ring, as gracefully as any soap bubble.

He picked himself up and bowed to the Emperor's screen.

"The earth-god is angry. Possibly there is something the matter with the salt," he said. "I do not think I shall wrestle this season." And he walked out, looking very suspiciously over one shoulder at Forever-Mountain.

Five other wrestlers then and there decided that they were not wrestling this season, either. They all looked annoyed with Forever-Mountain.

From then on, Forever-Mountain brought his foot down lightly. As each wrestler came into the ring, he picked him up very gently, carried him out, and placed him before the Emperor's screen, bowing most courteously every time.

The court ladies' eyebrows went up even higher. The gentlemen looked disturbed and a little afraid. They loved to see fierce, strong men tugging and grunting at each other, but Forever-Mountain was a little too much for them. Only the Emperor was happy behind his screen, for now, with the wrestling over so quickly, he would have that much more time to write his poems. He ordered all the prize money handed over to Forever-Mountain.

"But," he said, "you had better not wrestle any more." He stuck a finger through his screen and waggled it at the other wrestlers, who were sitting on the ground weeping with disappointment like great fat babies.

Forever-Mountain promised not to wrestle any more. Everybody looked relieved. The wrestlers sitting on the ground almost smiled.

"I think I shall become a farmer," Forever-Mountain said, and left at once to go back to Maru-me.

Maru-me was waiting for him. When she saw him coming, she ran down the mountain, picked him up, together with the heavy bags of prize money, and carried him halfway up the mountainside. Then she giggled and put him down. The rest of the way she let him carry her.

Forever-Mountain kept his promise to the Emperor and never fought in public again. His name was forgotten in the capital. But up in the mountains, sometimes, the earth shakes and rumbles, and they say that is Forever-Mountain and Maru-me's grandmother practicing wrestling in the hidden valley.

Claus Stamm

The Husband Who Was to Mind the House

Once on a time there was a man so surly and cross he never thought his Wife did anything right in the house. So, one evening in haymaking time, he came home, scolding and swearing, and showing his teeth, and making a dust.

"Dear love, don't be so angry; there's a good man," said his Goody. "Tomorrow let's change our work. I'll go out with the mowers and mow, and you shall mind the house at home."

Yes, the Husband thought, that would do very well.

So, early next morning his Goody took a scythe over her neck, went out into the hayfield with the mowers, and began to mow; the man was to mind the house and do the work at home.

First of all, he wanted to churn the butter; but when

he had churned a while, he got thirsty and went down to the cellar to tap a barrel of ale. So, just when he had knocked in the bung and was putting the tap into the cask, he heard overhead the pig come into the kitchen. Then off he ran as fast as he could up the cellar steps with the tap in his hand to look after the pig lest it should upset the churn; but when he got up and saw the pig had already knocked the churn over and stood there, rooting and grunting amongst the cream which was running all over the floor, he got so wild with rage that he quite forgot the ale barrel and ran at the pig as hard as he could. He caught it, too, just as it ran out of doors and gave it such a kick that piggy lay for dead on the spot. Then all at once he remembered he had the tap in his hand, but when he got down to the cellar, every drop of ale had run out of the cask.

Then he went into the dairy and found enough cream left to fill the churn again, and so he began to churn, for butter they must have at dinner. When he had churned a bit, he remembered that their milking cow was still shut up in the byre and hadn't a bite to eat or a drop to drink all the morning, though the sun was high. Then all at once he thought 'twas too far to take her down to the meadow, so he'd just get her up on the housetop — for the house, you must know, was thatched with sods, and a fine crop of grass was growing there. Now the house lay close up against a steep down, and he thought if he laid a plank across to the thatch at the back he'd easily get the cow up.

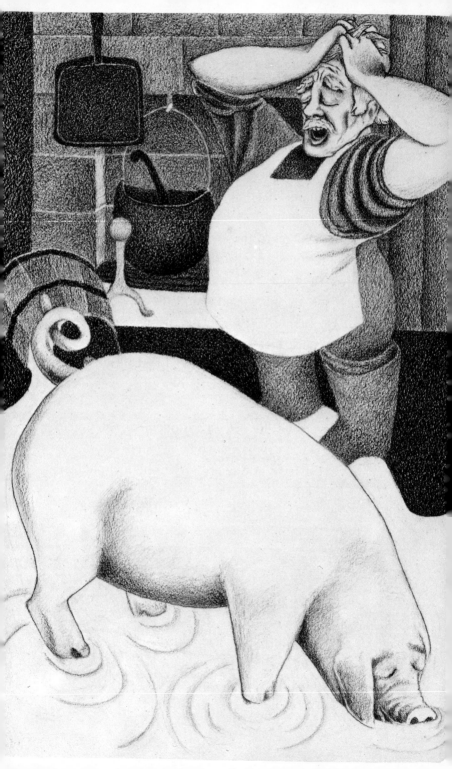

But still he couldn't leave the churn, for there was his little babe crawling about on the floor. "If I leave it," he thought, "the child is safe to upset it." So he took the churn on his back and went out with it; but then he thought he'd better first water the cow before he turned her out on the thatch. So he took up a bucket to draw water out of the well; but as he stooped down at the well's brink, all the cream ran out of the churn over his shoulders and so down into the well.

Now it was near dinner time, and he hadn't even got the butter yet; so he thought he'd best boil the porridge. He filled the pot with water and hung it over the fire. When he had done that, he thought the cow might perhaps fall off the thatch and break her legs or her neck. So he got up on the house to tie her up. One end of the rope he made fast to the cow's neck; the other he slipped down the chimney and tied round his own thigh. He had to make haste, for the water now began to boil in the pot, and he had still to grind the oatmeal.

So he began to grind away; but while he was hard at it, down fell the cow off the housetop after all, and as she fell, she dragged the man up the chimney by the rope. There he stuck fast. As for the cow, she hung halfway down the wall, swinging between heaven and earth, for she could neither get down nor up.

And now the Goody had waited seven lengths and seven breadths for her Husband to come and call her home to dinner; but never a call she had. At last she thought she'd waited long enough and went home. But

East of the Sun
and West of the Moon

Once on a time there was a poor husbandman who had so many children that he hadn't much of either food or clothing to give them. Pretty children they all were, but the prettiest was the youngest daughter, who was so lovely there was no end to her loveliness.

So one day — 'twas on a Thursday evening, late at the fall of the year — the weather was *so* wild and rough outside, and it was *so* cruelly dark, and rain fell and wind blew, till the walls of the cottage shook again. There they all sat round the fire, busy with this thing and that. But just then, all at once, something gave three taps on the windowpane. Then the father went out to see what was the matter; and when he got out of doors, what should he see but a great big White Bear.

"Good evening to you!" said the White Bear.

"The same to you," said the man.

"Will you give me your youngest daughter? If you will, I'll make you as rich as you are now poor," said the Bear.

Well, the man would not be at all sorry to be so rich, but still he thought he must have a bit of talk with his daughter first. So he went in and told them how there was a great White Bear waiting outside, who had given his word to make them so rich if he could only have the youngest daughter.

The lassie said "No!" outright. Nothing could get her to say anything else; so the man went out and settled it with the White Bear that he should come again the next Thursday evening and get an answer. Meantime he talked it over with his daughter and kept on telling her of all the riches they would get, and how well off she would be herself. So, at last she thought better of it and washed and mended her rags, made herself as smart as she could, and was ready to start. I can't say her packing gave her much trouble.

Next Thursday evening the White Bear came to fetch her. She got upon his back with her bundle, and off they went. So, when they had gone a bit of the way, the White Bear said: "Are you afraid?"

No, she wasn't.

"Well, mind and hold tight to my shaggy coat, and then there's nothing to fear," said the Bear.

So she rode a long, long way, till they came to a great steep hill. There, on the face of it, the White Bear gave a knock; a door opened, and they came into a castle where there were many rooms all lit up — rooms gleaming with silver and gold. There, too, was a table ready laid, and it was all as grand as grand could be. Then the White Bear gave her a silver bell. When she wanted anything, she was only to ring it, and she would get it at once.

Well, after she had eaten and drunk — and the evening wore on — she got sleepy after her journey, and thought she would like to go to bed. So she rang the bell; and she had scarce taken hold of it before she came into a chamber where there was a bed made, as fair and white as anyone would wish to sleep in, with silken pillows and curtains and gold fringe. All that was in the room was gold or silver. But when she had gone to bed and put out the light, a man came and laid himself alongside her. That was the White Bear, who threw off his beast shape at night; but she never saw him, for he always came after she had put out the light, and before the day dawned he was up and off again. So things went on happily for a while, but at last she began to get silent and sorrowful; for she went about all day alone, and she longed to go home to see her father and mother and brothers and sisters. So one day, when the White Bear asked what it was that she lacked, she said it was so dull and lonely there, and she longed to go home to see her father and mother and brothers and sisters, and she was so sad and sorrowful because she couldn't get to them.

"Well, well!" said the Bear, "perhaps there's a cure for all this; but you must promise me one thing: not to talk alone with your mother, but only when the rest are by to hear, for she'll take you by the hand and try to lead you into a room alone to talk. You must mind and not do that, else you'll bring bad luck on both of us."

So one Sunday the White Bear came and said now they could set off to see her father and mother. Well, off they started, she sitting on his back; and they went far and long. At last they came to a grand house. There her brothers and sisters were running about out of doors at play, and everything was so pretty, 'twas a joy to see.

"This is where your father and mother live now," said the White Bear; "but don't forget what I told you, else you'll make us both unlucky."

No! Bless her, she'd not forget — and when she had reached the house, the White Bear turned right about and left her.

Then, when she went in to see her father and mother, there was such joy, there was no end to it. None of them thought they could thank her enough for all she had done for them. Now they had everything they wished, as good as could be, and they all wanted to know how she got on where she lived.

Well, she said, it was very good to live where she

did; she had all she wished. What she said besides I don't know; but I don't think any of them had the right end of the stick, or that they got much out of her. But so, in the afternoon, after they had eaten dinner, all happened as the White Bear had said. Her mother wanted to talk with her alone in her bedroom, but she minded what the White Bear had said and wouldn't go upstairs.

"Oh, what we have to talk about will keep!" she said and put her mother off. But, somehow or other, her mother got round her at last, and she had to tell her the whole story. So she said how every night when she had gone to bed a man came and lay down beside her as soon as she had put out the light; how she never saw him, because he was always up and away before the morning dawned; how she went about woeful and sorrowing, for she thought she should so like to see him; how all day long she walked about there alone; and how dull and dreary and lonesome it was.

"My!" said her mother. "It may well be a troll you slept with! But now I'll teach you a lesson how to set eyes on him. I'll give you a bit of candle, which you can carry home in your bosom; just light that while he is asleep, but take care not to drop the tallow on him."

Yes, she took the candle and hid it in her bosom; and as night drew on, the White Bear came and fetched her away.

But when they had gone a bit of the way, the White Bear asked if all hadn't happened as he had said.

Well, she couldn't say it hadn't.

"Now, mind," said he, "if you have listened to your mother's advice, you have brought bad luck on us both; and then all that has passed between us will be as nothing."

No, she said, she hadn't listened to her mother's advice.

So when she reached home and had gone to bed, it was the same old story over again. There came a man who lay down beside her; but at dead of night, when she heard he slept, she got up and struck a light, lit the candle, and let the light shine on him. And so she saw that he was the loveliest Prince one ever set eyes on, and she fell so deep in love with him on the spot that she thought she couldn't live if she didn't give him a kiss there and then. And so she did; but as she kissed him, she dropped three hot drops of tallow on his shirt, and he woke up.

"What have you done?" he cried. "Now you have made us both unlucky, for had you held out only this one year, I would have been freed. For I have a stepmother who has bewitched me, so that I am a White Bear by day and a man by night. But now all ties are snapped between us; now I must set off from you to her. She lives in a castle which stands east of the sun and west of the moon; and there, too, is a Princess, with a nose three ells long. She's the wife I must have now."

She wept and took it ill, but there was no help for it. Go he must.

Then she asked if she mightn't go with him?

No, she mightn't.

"Tell me the way, then," she said, "and I'll search you out; *that* surely I may get leave to do."

Yes, she might do that, he said; but there was no way to that place. It lay east of the sun and west of the moon, and thither she'd never find her way.

So next morning when she woke up, both Prince and castle were gone. She lay on a little green patch, in the midst of the gloomy thick wood, and by her side lay the same bundle of rags she had brought with her from her old home.

So when she had rubbed the sleep out of her eyes and wept till she was tired, she set out on her way. She walked many, many days, till she came to a lofty crag. Under it sat an old hag, who played with a gold apple which she tossed about. The lassie asked her if she knew the way to the Prince, who lived with his step-mother in the castle that lay east of the sun and west of the moon, and who was to marry the Princess with a nose three ells long.

"How did you come to know about him?" asked the old hag. "But maybe you are the lassie who ought to have had him?"

Yes, she was.

"So, so; it's you, is it?" said the old hag. "Well, all I know about him is that he lives in the castle that lies east of the sun and west of the moon, and thither you'll come, late or never. But still you may have the loan of my horse, and on him you can ride to my next neighbor.

Maybe she'll be able to tell you; and when you get there, just give the horse a switch under the left ear and beg him to be off home. And, stay, this gold apple you may take with you.''

So she got upon the horse and rode a long, long time, till she came to another crag, under which sat another old hag with a gold carding-comb. The lassie asked her if she knew the way to the castle that lay east of the sun and west of the moon. She answered, like the first old hag, that she knew nothing about it, except it was east of the sun and west of the moon.

''And thither you'll come, late or never, but you shall have the loan of my horse to my next neighbor. Maybe she'll tell you all about it; and when you get there, just switch the horse under the left ear and beg him to be off home.''

And this old hag gave her the golden carding-comb. It might be she'd find some use for it, she said. So the lassie got upon the horse and rode a far, far way and a weary time. So at last she came to another great crag, under which sat another old hag, spinning with a golden spinning wheel. She asked her, too, if she knew the way to the Prince and where the castle was that lay east of the sun and west of the moon. So it was the same thing over again.

''Maybe it's you who ought to have had the Prince?'' said the old hag.

Yes, it was.

But she didn't know the way a bit better than the

other two. East of the sun and west of the moon it was, she knew — that was all.

"And thither you'll come, late or never; but I'll lend you my horse, and then I think you'd best ride to the East Wind and ask him. Maybe he knows those parts and can blow you thither. But when you get to him, you need only give the horse a switch under the left ear, and he'll trot home of himself."

And so, too, she gave her the gold spinning wheel. "Maybe you'll find a use for it," said the old hag.

Then on she rode many, many days, a weary time, before she got to the East Wind's house; but at last she did reach it, and then she asked the East Wind if he could tell her the way to the Prince who dwelt east of the sun and west of the moon. Yes, the East Wind had often heard tell of it, the Prince and the castle, but he couldn't tell the way, for he had never blown so far.

"But, if you will, I'll go with you to my brother the West Wind. Maybe he knows, for he's much stronger. So, if you will just get on my back, I'll carry you thither."

Yes, she got on his back, and I should think they went briskly along.

When they got there, they went into the West Wind's house, and the East Wind said the lassie he had brought was the one who ought to have had the Prince who lived in the castle east of the sun and west of the moon; and so she had set out to seek him, and how he had come with her, and would be glad to know if the West Wind knew how to get to the castle.

"Nay," said the West Wind, "so far I've never blown; but if you will, I'll go with you to our brother the South Wind, for he's much stronger than either of us, and he has flapped his wings far and wide. Maybe he'll tell you. You can get on my back, and I'll carry you to him."

Yes, she got on his back, and they traveled to the South Wind. They weren't so very long on the way, I should think.

When they got there, the West Wind asked him if he could tell her the way to the castle that lay east of the sun and west of the moon, for it was she who ought to have had the Prince who lived there.

"You don't say so! That's she, is it?" said the South Wind.

"Well, I have blustered about in most places in my time, but so far have I never blown; but if you will, I'll take you to my brother the North Wind. He is the oldest and strongest of the whole lot of us, and if he doesn't know where it is, you'll never find anyone in the world to tell you. You can get on my back, and I'll carry you thither."

Yes, she got on his back, and away he went at a fine rate. And this time, too, she wasn't long on her way.

When they got to the North Wind's house, he was so wild and cross, cold puffs came from him a long way off.

"BLAST YOU BOTH, WHAT DO YOU WANT?"
he roared out to them ever so far off, so that it struck
them with an icy shiver.

"Well," said the South Wind, "you needn't be so
very nasty, for here I am, your brother the South Wind,
and here is the lassie who ought to have had the Prince
who dwells in the castle that lies east of the sun and
west of the moon. She wants to ask you if you ever
were there and can tell her the way, for she would be so
glad to find him again."

"YES, I KNOW WELL ENOUGH WHERE IT IS,"
shouted the North Wind. "Once in my life I blew an
aspen leaf thither, but I was so tired that I couldn't blow
a puff for ever so many days after. But if you really
wish to go thither and aren't afraid to come along with
me, I'll take you on my back and see if I can blow you
thither."

Yes, with all her heart; she must and would get
thither if it were possible in any way. As for fear, however madly he went, she wouldn't be at all afraid.

"Very well, then," said the North Wind; "but you
must sleep here tonight, for we must have the whole day
before us if we're to get thither at all."

Early next morning the North Wind woke her, and
puffed himself up, and blew himself out, and made himself so stout and big 'twas gruesome to look at him.
Off they went high up through the air, as if they would
never stop till they got to the world's end.

Down here below there was such a storm it threw

down long tracts of wood and many houses, and when it swept over the great sea, ships foundered by hundreds.

So they tore on and on — no one can believe how far they went — and all the while they still went over the sea. The North Wind got more and more weary and so out of breath he could scarce bring out a puff; his wings drooped and drooped, till at last he sank so low that the crests of the waves dashed over his heels.

"Are you afraid?" said the North Wind.

No, she wasn't.

But they weren't very far from land, and the North Wind had still so much strength left in him that he managed to throw her up on the shore under the windows of the castle which lay east of the sun and west of the moon. But then he was so weak and worn out, he had to stay there and rest many days before he could get home again.

Next morning the lassie sat down under the castle window and began to play with the gold apple, and the first person she saw was the Long-Nose who was to have the Prince.

"What do you want for your gold apple, you lassie?" said the Long-Nose, throwing open the window.

"It's not for sale, for gold or money," said the lassie.

"If it's not for sale for gold or money, what is it that you will sell it for? You may name your own price," said the Princess.

"Well, if I may get to the Prince, who lives here, and

be with him tonight, you shall have it,'' said the lassie whom the North Wind had brought.

Yes, she might; that could be done. So the Princess got the gold apple, but when the lassie came up to the Prince's bedroom at night he was fast asleep. She called him and shook him, and between whiles she wept sore; but for all she could do she couldn't wake him up. Next morning, as soon as day broke, the Princess with the long nose came and drove her out again.

So in the daytime she sat down under the castle windows and began to card with her carding-comb, and the same thing happened. The Princess asked what she wanted for it; and she said it wasn't for sale for gold or money, but if she might get leave to go up to the Prince and be with him that night, the Princess should have it. But when she went up she found him fast asleep again, and for all she called, and for all she shook, and wept, and prayed, she couldn't get life into him. As soon as the first gray peep of day came, then came the Princess with the long nose and chased her out again.

So, in the daytime, the lassie sat down outside under the castle window and began to spin with her golden spinning wheel; that, too, the Princess with the long nose wanted to have. So she threw open the window and asked what the lassie wanted for it. The lassie said, as she had said twice before, it wasn't for sale for gold or money; but if she might go up to the Prince who was there, and be with him alone that night, the Princess might have it.

Yes, she might do that and welcome. But now you must know there were some Christian folk who had been carried off thither. As they sat in their room, which was next to the Prince's, they had heard a woman in there, weeping and praying, and calling to him two nights running; and they told that to the Prince.

That evening when the Princess came with her sleepy drink, the Prince pretended to drink, but threw it over his shoulder, for he could guess it was a sleepy drink. So, when the lassie came in, she found the Prince wide awake. Then she told him the whole story of how she had come thither.

"Ah," said the Prince, "you've just come in the very nick of time, for tomorrow is to be our wedding day; but now I won't have the Long-Nose, and you are the only woman in the world who can set me free. I'll say I want to see what my wife is fit for and beg her to wash the shirt which has the three spots of tallow on it. She'll say yes, for she doesn't know 'tis you who put them there. That's a work only for Christian folk, and not for such a pack of trolls, and so I'll say that I won't have any other for my bride than the woman who can wash them out. Then I'll ask you to do it."

So there was great joy and love between them all that night. But next day, when the wedding was to be, the Prince said: "First of all, I'd like to see what my bride is fit for."

"Yes," said the stepmother, with all her heart.

"Well," said the Prince, "I've got a fine shirt which I'd like for my wedding shirt, but somehow or other it has got three spots of tallow on it, which I must have washed out. I have sworn never to take any other bride than the woman who's able to do that. If she can't, she's not worth having."

Well, that was no great thing, they said; so they agreed. She with the long nose began to wash away as hard as she could, but the more she rubbed and scrubbed, the bigger the spots grew.

"Ah!" said the old hag, her mother, "you can't wash. Let me try."

But she hadn't long taken the shirt in hand before it got far worse than ever, and with all her rubbing and wringing and scrubbing, the spots grew bigger and blacker; and the darker and uglier was the shirt.

Then all the other trolls began to wash; but the longer it lasted, the blacker and uglier the shirt grew, till at last it was as black all over as if it had been up the chimney.

"Ah!" said the Prince, "you're none of you worth a straw. You can't wash. Why there, outside, sits a beggar lassie. I'll be bound she knows how to wash better than the whole lot of you. COME IN, LASSIE!" he shouted.

Well, in she came.

"Can you wash this shirt clean, lassie you?" said he.

"I don't know," she said, "but I think I can."

And almost before she had taken it and dipped it in the water, it was as white as driven snow, and whiter still.

"Yes; you are the lassie for me," said the Prince.

At that the old hag flew into such a rage, she burst on the spot, and the Princess with the long nose after her, and the whole pack of trolls after her — at least I've never heard a word about them since.

As for the Prince and Princess, they set free all the poor Christian folk who had been carried off and shut up there; and they took with them all the silver and gold and flitted away as far as they could from the castle that lay east of the sun and west of the moon.

Asbjörnsen and Moe

Unanana
and the Elephant

Many, many years ago there was a woman called
Unanana who had two beautiful children. They lived in
a hut near the roadside and people passing by would
often stop when they saw the children, exclaiming at the
roundness of their limbs, the smoothness of their skin
and the brightness of their eyes.

Early one morning Unanana went into the bush to
collect firewood and left her two children playing with a
little cousin who was living with them. The children
shouted happily, seeing who could jump the furthest,
and when they were tired they sat on the dusty ground
outside the hut, playing a game with pebbles.

Suddenly they heard a rustle in the nearby grasses,
and seated on a rock they saw a puzzled-looking baboon.

'Whose children are those?' he asked the little cousin.

'They belong to Unanana,' she replied.

'Well, well, well!' exclaimed the baboon in his deep voice. 'Never have I seen such beautiful children before.'

Then he disappeared and the children went on with their game.

A little later they heard the faint crack of a twig and looking up they saw the big, brown eyes of a gazelle staring at them from beside a bush.

'Whose children are those?' she asked the cousin.

'They belong to Unanana,' she replied.

'Well, well, well!' exclaimed the gazelle in her soft, smooth voice. 'Never have I seen such beautiful children before,' and with a graceful bound she disappeared into the bush.

The children grew tired of their game, and taking a small gourd they dipped it in turn into the big pot full of water which stood at the door of their hut, and drank their fill.

A sharp bark made the cousin drop her gourd in fear when she looked up and saw the spotted body and treacherous eyes of a leopard, who had crept silently out of the bush.

'Whose children are those?' he demanded.

'They belong to Unanana,' she replied in a shaky voice, slowly backing towards the door of the hut in case the leopard should spring at her. But he was not interested in a meal just then.

'Never have I seen such beautiful children before,' he exclaimed, and with a flick of his tail he melted away into the bush.

The children were afraid of all these animals who kept asking questions and called loudly to Unanana to return, but instead of their mother, a huge elephant with only one tusk lumbered out of the bush and stood staring at the three children, who were too frightened to move.

'Whose children are those?' he bellowed at the little cousin, waving his trunk in the direction of the two beautiful children who were trying to hide behind a large stone.

'They . . . they belong to Una . . . Unanana,' faltered the little girl.

The elephant took a step forward.

'Never have I seen such beautiful children before,' he boomed. 'I will take them away with me,' and opening wide his mouth he swallowed both children at a gulp.

The little cousin screamed in terror and dashed into the hut, and from the gloom and safety inside it she heard the elephant's heavy footsteps growing fainter and fainter as he went back into the bush.

It was not until much later that Unanana returned, carrying a large bundle of wood on her head. The little girl rushed out of the house in a dreadful state and it was some time before Unanana could get the whole story from her.

'Alas! Alas!' said the mother. 'Did he swallow them

whole? Do you think they might still be alive inside the elephant's stomach?'

'I cannot tell,' said the child, and she began to cry even louder than before.

'Well,' said Unanana sensibly, 'there's only one thing to do. I must go into the bush and ask all the animals whether they have seen an elephant with only one tusk. But first of all I must make preparations.'

She took a pot and cooked a lot of beans in it until they were soft and ready to eat. Then seizing her large knife and putting the pot of food on her head, she told her little niece to look after the hut until she returned, and set off into the bush to search for the elephant.

Unanana soon found the tracks of the huge beast and followed them for some distance, but the elephant himself was nowhere to be seen. Presently, as she passed through some tall, shady trees, she met the baboon.

'O baboon! Do help me!' she begged. 'Have you seen an elephant with only one tusk? He has eaten both my children and I must find him.'

'Go straight along this track until you come to a place where there are high trees and white stones. There you will find the elephant,' said the baboon.

So the woman went on along the dusty track for a very long time but she saw no sign of the elephant.

Suddenly she noticed a gazelle leaping across her path.

'O gazelle! Do help me! Have you seen an elephant

with only one tusk?' she asked. 'He has eaten both my children and I must find him.'

'Go straight along this track until you come to a place where there are high trees and white stones. There you will find the elephant,' said the gazelle, as she bounded away.

'O dear!' sighed Unanana. 'It seems a very long way and I am so tired and hungry.'

But she did not eat the food she carried, since that was for her children when she found them.

On and on she went, until rounding a bend in the track she saw a leopard sitting outside his cave-home, washing himself with his tongue.

'O leopard!' she exclaimed in a tired voice. 'Do help me! Have you seen an elephant with only one tusk? He has eaten both my children and I must find him.'

'Go straight along this track until you come to a place where there are high trees and white stones. There you will find the elephant,' replied the leopard, as he bent his head and continued his toilet.

'Alas!' gasped Unanana to herself. 'If I do not find this place soon, my legs will carry me no further.'

She staggered on a little further until suddenly, ahead of her, she saw some high trees with large white stones spread about on the ground below them.

'At last!' she exclaimed, and hurrying forward she found a huge elephant lying contentedly in the shade of the trees. One glance was enough to show her that he had only one tusk, so going up as close as she dared, she shouted angrily:

'Elephant! Elephant! Are you the one that has eaten my children?'

'O no!' he replied lazily. 'Go straight along this track until you come to a place where there are high trees and white stones. There you will find the elephant.'

But the woman was sure this was the elephant she sought, and stamping her foot, she screamed at him again:

'Elephant! Elephant! Are you the one that has eaten my children?'

'O no! Go straight along this track — ' began the elephant again, but he was cut short by Unanana who rushed up to him waving her knife and yelling:

'Where are my children? Where are they?'

Then the elephant opened his mouth and without even troubling to stand up, he swallowed Unanana with the cooking-pot and her knife at one gulp. And this was just what Unanana had hoped for.

Down, down, down she went in the darkness, until she reached the elephant's stomach. What a sight met her eyes! The walls of the elephant's stomach were like a range of hills, and camped among these hills were little groups of people, many dogs and goats and cows, and her own two beautiful children.

'Mother! Mother!' they cried when they saw her. 'How did you get here? Oh, we are so hungry.'

Unanana took the cooking-pot off her head and began

to feed her children with the beans, which they ate rav-
enously. All the other people crowded round, begging
for just a small portion of the food, so Unanana said to
them scornfully:

'Why do you not roast meat for yourselves, seeing
that you are surrounded by it?'

She took her knife and cut large pieces of flesh from
the elephant and roasted them over a fire she built in the
middle of the elephant's stomach, and soon everyone,
including the dogs and goats and cattle, was feasting on
elephant-meat very happily.

But the groans of the poor elephant could be heard all
over the bush, and he said to those animals who came
along to find out the cause of his unhappiness:

'I don't know why it is, but ever since I swallowed
that woman called Unanana, I have felt most uncomfort-
able and unsettled inside.'

The pain got worse and worse, until with a final grunt
the elephant dropped dead. Then Unanana seized her
knife again and hacked a doorway between the elephant's ribs through which soon streamed a line of dogs,
goats, cows, men, women and children, all blinking
their eyes in the strong sunlight and shouting for joy at
being free once more.

The animals barked, bleated or mooed their thanks,
while the human beings gave Unanana all kinds of
presents in gratitude to her for setting them free, so that
when Unanana and her two children reached home, they
were no longer poor.

The little cousin was delighted to see them, for she had thought they were all dead, and that night they had a feast. Can you guess what they ate? Yes, roasted elephant-meat.

Kathleen Arnott

The Woman Who Flummoxed the Fairies

There was a woman once who was a master baker. Her bannocks were like wheaten cakes, her wheaten cakes were like the finest pastries, and her pastries were like nothing but Heaven itself in the mouth!

Not having her match, or anything like it, in seven counties round she made a good penny by it, for there wasn't a wedding nor a christening for miles around in the countryside but she was called upon to make the cakes for it, and she got all the trade of all the gentry as well. She was fair in her prices and she was honest, too, but she was that goodhearted into the bargain. Those who could pay well she charged aplenty, but when some poor body came and begged her to make a wee bit of a cake for a celebration and timidly offered her the little money they had for it, she'd wave it away and tell them to pay her when they got the cake. Then she'd set to and bake a cake as fine and big as any she'd make for a laird, and she'd send it to them as a gift, with the best respects of her husband and herself, to the wedding pair or the parents of the baby that was to be christened, so nobody's feelings were hurt.

Not only was she a master baker, but she was the cleverest woman in the world; and it was the first that got her into trouble, but it was the second that got her out of it.

The fairies have their own good foods to eat, but they dearly love a bit of baker's cake once in a while, and will often steal a slice of one by night from a kitchen while all the folks in a house are sleeping.

In a nearby hill there was a place where the fairies lived, and of all cakes the ones the fairies liked best were the ones this master baker made. The trouble was, the taste of one was hard to come by, for her cakes were all so good that they were always eaten up at a sitting, with hardly a crumb left over for a poor fairy to find.

So then the fairies plotted together to carry the woman away and to keep her with them always just to bake cakes for them.

Their chance came not long after, for there was to be a great wedding at the castle with hundreds of guests invited, and the woman was to make the cakes. There would have to be so many of them, with so many people coming to eat them, that the woman was to spend the whole day before the wedding in the castle kitchen doing nothing but baking one cake after another!

The fairies learned about this from one of their number who had been listening at the keyhole of the baker's door. They found out, too, what road she'd be taking coming home.

When the night came, there they were by a fairy mound where the road went by, hiding in flower cups, and under leaves, and in all manner of places.

When she came by they all flew out at her. "The fireflies are gey thick the night," said she. But it was not fireflies. It was fairies with the moonlight sparkling on their wings.

Then the fairies drifted fern seed into her eyes, and all of a sudden she was that sleepy that she could go not one step farther without a bit of a rest!

"Mercy me!" she said with a yawn. "It's worn myself out I have this day!" And she sank down on what she took to be a grassy bank to doze just for a minute. But it wasn't a bank at all. It was the fairy mound, and once she lay upon it she was in the fairies' power.

She knew nothing about that nor anything else till she woke again, and found herself in fairyland. Being a clever woman she didn't have to be told where she was, and she guessed how she got there. But she didn't let on.

"Well now," she said happily, "and did you ever! It's all my life I've wanted to get a peep into fairyland. And here I am!"

They told her what they wanted, and she said to herself, indeed she had no notion of staying there the rest of her life! But she didn't tell the fairies that either.

"To be sure!" she said cheerfully. "Why you poor wee things! To think of me baking cakes for everyone else, and not a one for you! So let's be at it," said she, "with no time wasted."

Then from her kittiebag that hung at her side she took a clean apron and tied it around her waist, while the fairies, happy that she was so willing, licked their lips in anticipation and rubbed their hands for joy.

"Let me see now," said she, looking about her. "Well, 'tis plain you have nothing for me to be baking a cake with. You'll just have to be going to my own kitchen to fetch back what I'll need."

Yes, the fairies could do that. So she sent some for eggs, and some for sugar, and some for flour, and some for butter, while others flew off to get a wheen of other things she told them she had to have. At last all was ready for the mixing and the woman asked for a bowl. But the biggest one they could find for her was the size of a teacup, and a wee dainty one at that.

Well then, there was nothing for it, but they must go and fetch her big yellow crockery bowl from off the shelf over the water butt. And after that it was her wooden spoons and her egg whisp and one thing and another, till the fairies were all fagged out, what with the flying back and forth, and the carrying, and only the thought of the cake to come of it kept their spirits up at all.

At last everything she wanted was at hand. The woman began to measure and mix and whip and beat. But all of a sudden she stopped.

" 'Tis no use!'' she sighed. "I can't ever seem to mix a cake without my cat beside me, purring.''

"Fetch the cat!'' said the fairy king sharply.

So they fetched the cat. The cat lay at the woman's feet and purred, and the woman stirred away at the bowl, and for a while all was well. But not for long.

The woman let go of the spoon and sighed again. "Well now, would you think it?'' said she. "I'm that used to my dog setting the time of my beating by the way he snores at every second beat that I can't seem to get the beat right without him.''

"Fetch the dog!'' cried the king.

So they fetched the dog and he curled up at her feet beside the cat. The dog snored, the cat purred, the woman beat the cake batter, and all was well again. Or so the fairies thought.

But no! The woman stopped again. "I'm that worried about my babe,'' said she. "Away from him all night as I've been, and him with a new tooth pushing through this very week. It seems I just can't mix . . .''

"Fetch that babe!'' roared the fairy king, without

waiting for her to finish what she was saying. And they fetched the babe.

So the woman began to beat the batter again. But when they brought the babe, he began to scream the minute he saw her, for he was hungry, as she knew he would be, because he never would let his dadda feed him his porridge and she had not been home to do it.

"I'm sorry to trouble you," said the woman, raising her voice above the screaming of the babe, "but I can't stop beating now lest the cake go wrong. Happen my husband could get the babe quiet if . . ."

The fairies didn't wait for the king to tell them what to do. Off they flew and fetched the husband back with them. He, poor man, was all in a whirl, what with things disappearing from under his eyes right and left, and then being snatched through the air himself the way he was. But here was his wife, and he knew where she was things couldn't go far wrong. But the baby went on screaming.

So the woman beat the batter, and the baby screamed, and the cat purred, and the dog snored, and the man rubbed his eyes and watched his wife to see what she was up to. The fairies settled down, though 'twas plain to see that the babe's screaming disturbed them. Still, they looked hopeful.

Then the woman reached over and took up the egg whisp and gave the wooden spoon to the babe, who at once began to bang away with it, screaming just the same. Under cover of the screaming of the babe and

the banging of the spoon and the swishing of the egg
whisp the woman whispered to her husband, ''Pinch the
dog!''

''What?'' said the man. But he did it just the
same — and kept on doing it.

''Tow! Row! Row!'' barked the dog, and added his
voice to the babe's screams, and the banging of the
wooden spoon, and the swishing of the egg whisp.

''Tread on the tail of the cat!'' whispered the woman
to her husband, and it's a wonder he could hear her.
But he did. He had got the notion now and he entered
the game for himself. He not only trod on the tail of the
cat, but he kept his foot there while the cat howled like
a dozen lost souls.

So the woman swished, and the baby screamed, and
the wooden spoon banged, and the dog yelped, and the
cat howled, and the whole of it made a terrible din.
The fairies, king and all, flew round and round in dis-
traction with their hands over their ears, for if there is
one thing the fairies can't bear it's a lot of noise and
there was a lot more than a lot of noise in fairyland that
day! And what's more the woman knew what they
liked and what they didn't all the time!

So then the woman got up and poured the batter into
two pans that stood ready. She laid by the egg whisp
and took the wooden spoon away from the babe, and
picking him up she popped a lump of sugar into his
mouth. That surprised him so much that he stopped
screaming. She nodded to her husband and he stopped

pinching the dog and took his foot from the cat's tail, and in a minute's time all was quiet. The fairies stopped flying round and round and sank down exhausted.

And then the woman said, "The cake's ready for the baking. Where's the oven?"

The fairies looked at each other in dismay, and at last the fairy queen said weakly, "There isn't any oven."

"What!" exclaimed the woman. "No oven? Well then, how do you expect me to be baking the cake?"

None of the fairies could find the answer to that.

"Well then," said the woman, "you'll just have to be taking me and the cake home to bake it in my own oven, and bring me back later when the cake's all done."

The fairies looked at the babe and the wooden spoon and the egg whisp and the dog and the cat and the man. And then they all shuddered like one.

"You may all go!" said the fairy king. "But don't ask us to be taking you. We're all too tired."

"Och, you must have your cake then," said the woman, feeling sorry for them now she'd got what she wanted, which was to go back to her own home, "after all the trouble you've had for it! I'll tell you what I'll do. After it's baked, I'll be leaving it for you beside the road, behind the bank where you found me. And what's more I'll put one there for you every single week's end from now on."

The thought of having one of the woman's cakes

every week revived the fairies so that they forgot they were all worn out. Or almost did.

"I'll not be outdone!" cried the fairy king. "For what you find in that same place shall be your own!"

Then the woman picked up the pans of batter, and the man tucked the bowls and spoons and things under one arm and the baby under the other. The fairy king raised an arm and the hill split open. Out they all walked, the woman with the pans of batter, the man with the bowls and the babe, and the dog and the cat at their heels. Down the road they walked and back to their own house, and never looked behind them.

When they got back to their home the woman put the pans of batter into the oven, and then she dished out the porridge that stood keeping hot on the back of the fire and gave the babe his supper.

There wasn't a sound in that house except for the clock ticking and the kettle singing and the cat purring and the dog snoring. And all those were soft, quiet sounds.

"I'll tell you what," said the man at last. "It doesn't seem fair on the rest of the men that I should have the master baker and the cleverest woman in the world all in one wife."

"Trade me off then for one of the ordinary kind," said his wife, laughing at him.

"I'll not do it," said he. "I'm very well suited as I am."

So that's the way the woman flummoxed the fairies.

A good thing she made out of it, too, for when the cake was baked and cooled the woman took it up and put it behind the fairy mound, as she had promised. And when she set it down she saw there a little brown bag. She took the bag up and opened it and looked within, and it was full of bright shining yellow gold pieces.

And so it went, week after week. A cake for the fairies, a bag of gold for the woman and her husband. They never saw one of the fairies again, but the bargain never was broken and they grew rich by it. So of course they lived, as why should they not, happily ever after.

Sorche Nic Leodhas

Clever Manka

There was once a rich farmer who was as grasping and unscrupulous as he was rich. He was always driving a hard bargain and always getting the better of his poor neighbors. One of these neighbors was a humble shepherd who, in return for service, was to receive from the farmer a heifer. When the time of payment came, the farmer refused to give the shepherd the heifer, and the shepherd was forced to lay the matter before the burgomaster.

The burgomaster, who was a young man and as yet not very experienced, listened to both sides, and when he had deliberated, he said:

"Instead of deciding this case, I will put a riddle to you both, and the man who makes the best answer shall have the heifer. Are you agreed?"

The farmer and the shepherd accepted this proposal and the burgomaster said:

"Well, then, here is my riddle: What is the swiftest thing in the world? What is the sweetest thing? What is the richest? Think out your answers and bring them to me at this same hour tomorrow."

The farmer went home in a temper.

"What kind of burgomaster is this young fellow!" he growled. "If he had let me keep the heifer, I'd have sent him a bushel of pears. But now I'm in a fair way of losing the heifer, for I can't think of any answer to his foolish riddle."

"What is the matter, husband?" his wife asked.

"It's that new burgomaster. The old one would have given me the heifer without any argument, but this young man thinks to decide the case by asking us riddles."

When he told his wife what the riddle was, she cheered him greatly by telling him that she knew the answers at once.

"Why, husband," said she, "our gray mare must be the swiftest thing in the world. You know yourself nothing ever passes us on the road. As for the sweetest, did you ever taste honey any sweeter than ours? And I'm sure there's nothing richer than our chest of golden ducats that we've been laying by these forty years."

The farmer was delighted.

"You're right, wife, you're right! That heifer remains ours!"

The shepherd, when he got home, was downcast and sad. He had a daughter, a clever girl named Manka, who met him at the door of his cottage and asked:

"What is it, father? What did the burgomaster say?"

The shepherd sighed.

"I'm afraid I've lost the heifer. The burgomaster set us a riddle, and I know I shall never guess it."

"Perhaps I can help you," Manka said. "What is it?"

The shepherd gave her the riddle, and the next day, as he was setting out for the burgomaster's, Manka told him what answers to make.

When he reached the burgomaster's house, the farmer was already there rubbing his hands and beaming with self-importance.

The burgomaster again propounded the riddle and then asked the farmer his answers.

The farmer cleared his throat and with a pompous air began:

"The swiftest thing in the world? Why, my dear sir, that's my gray mare, of course, for no other horse ever passes us on the road. The sweetest? Honey from my beehives, to be sure. The richest? What can be richer than my chest of golden ducats!"

And the farmer squared his shoulders and smiled triumphantly.

"H'm," said the young burgomaster dryly. Then he asked:

"What answers does the shepherd make?"

The shepherd bowed politely and said:

"The swiftest thing in the world is thought, for thought can run any distance in the twinkling of an eye. The sweetest thing of all is sleep, for when a man is tired and sad; what can be sweeter? The richest thing is the earth, for out of the earth come all the riches of the world."

"Good!" the burgomaster cried. "Good! The heifer goes to the shepherd!"

Later the burgomaster said to the shepherd:

"Tell me now, who gave you those answers? I'm sure they never came out of your own head."

At first the shepherd tried not to tell, but when the burgomaster pressed him, he confessed that they came from his daughter, Manka. The burgomaster, who thought he would like to make another test of Manka's cleverness, sent for ten eggs. He gave them to the shepherd and said:

"Take these eggs to Manka and tell her to have them hatched out by tomorrow and to bring me the chicks."

When the shepherd reached home and gave Manka the burgomaster's message, Manka laughed and said: "Take a handful of millet and go right back to the burgomaster. Say to him: 'My daughter sends you this millet. She says that if you plant it, grow it, and have it harvested by tomorrow, she'll bring you the ten chicks and you can feed them the ripe grain.'"

When the burgomaster heard this, he laughed heartily.

"That's a clever girl of yours," he told the shepherd. "If she's as comely as she is clever, I think I'd like to marry her. Tell her to come to see me, but she must come neither by day nor by night, neither riding nor walking, neither dressed nor undressed."

When Manka received this message, she waited until the next dawn when night was gone and day not yet arrived. Then she wrapped herself in a fish net and, throwing one leg over a goat's back and keeping one foot on the ground, she went to the burgomaster's house.

Now I ask you: did she go dressed? No, she wasn't dressed. A fish net isn't clothing. Did she go undressed? Of course not, for wasn't she covered with a fish net? Did she walk to the burgomaster's? No, she didn't walk, for she went with one leg thrown over a goat. Then did she ride? Of course she didn't ride, for wasn't she walking on one foot?

When she reached the burgomaster's house, she called out:

"Here I am, Mr. Burgomaster, and I've come neither by day nor by night, neither riding nor walking, neither dressed nor undressed."

The young burgomaster was so delighted with Manka's cleverness and so pleased with her comely looks that he proposed to her at once and in a short time married her.

"But understand, my dear Manka," he said, "you are not to use that cleverness of yours at my expense. I

won't have you interfering in any of my cases. In fact, if ever you give advice to anyone who comes to me for judgment, I'll turn you out of my house at once and send you home to your father.''

All went well for a time. Manka busied herself in her housekeeping and was careful not to interfere in any of the burgomaster's cases.

Then one day two farmers came to the burgomaster to have a dispute settled. One of the farmers owned a mare that had foaled in the marketplace. The colt had run under the wagon of the other farmer, and thereupon the owner of the wagon claimed the colt as his property.

The burgomaster, who was thinking of something else while the case was being presented, said carelessly:

''The man who found the colt under his wagon is, of course, the owner of the colt.''

As the owner of the mare was leaving the burgomaster's house, he met Manka and stopped to tell her about the case. Manka was ashamed of her husband for making so foolish a decision, and she said to the farmer:

''Come back this afternoon with a fishing net and stretch it across the dusty road. When the burgomaster sees you, he will come out and ask you what you are doing. Say to him that you're catching fish. When he asks you how you can expect to catch fish in a dusty road, tell him it's just as easy for you to catch fish in a dusty road as it is for a wagon to foal. Then he'll see the injustice of his decision and have the colt returned to you. But remember one thing: you mustn't let him find out that it was I who told you to do this.''

That afternoon, when the burgomaster chanced to look out the window, he saw a man stretching a fish net across the dusty road. He went out to him and asked:

''What are you doing?''

''Fishing.''

''Fishing in a dusty road? Are you daft?''

''Well,'' the man said, ''it's just as easy for me to catch fish in a dusty road as it is for a wagon to foal.''

Then the burgomaster recognized the man as the owner of the mare, and he had to confess that what he said was true.

''Of course the colt belongs to your mare and must be returned to you. But tell me,'' he said, ''who put you up to this? You didn't think of it yourself.''

The farmer tried not to tell, but the burgomaster questioned him until he found out that Manka was at the bottom of it. This made him very angry. He went into the house and called his wife.

''Manka,'' he said, ''did you forget what I told you would happen if you went interfering in any of my cases? Home you go this very day. I don't care to hear any excuses. The matter is settled. You may take with you the one thing you like best in my house, for I won't have people saying that I treated you shabbily.''

Manka made no outcry.

''Very well, my dear husband, I shall do as you say: I

shall go home to my father's cottage and take with me the one thing I like best in your house. But don't make me go until after supper. We have been very happy together and I should like to eat one last meal with you. Let us have no more words but be kind to each other as we've always been and then part as friends.''

The burgomaster agreed to this, and Manka prepared a fine supper of all the dishes of which her husband was particularly fond. The burgomaster opened his choicest wine and pledged Manka's health. Then he set to, and the supper was so good that he ate and ate and ate. And the more he ate, the more he drank until at last he grew drowsy and fell sound asleep in his chair. Then without awakening him, Manka had him carried out to the wagon that was waiting to take her home to her father.

The next morning, when the burgomaster opened his eyes, he found himself lying in the shepherd's cottage.

"What does this mean?" he roared out.

"Nothing, dear husband, nothing!" Manka said. "You know you told me I might take with me the one thing I liked best in your house, so of course I took you! That's all."

For a moment the burgomaster rubbed his eyes in amazement. Then he laughed loud and heartily to think how Manka had outwitted him.

"Manka," he said, "you're too clever for me. Come on, my dear, let's go home."

So, they climbed back into the wagon and drove home.

The burgomaster never again scolded his wife, but thereafter whenever a very difficult case came up, he always said:

"I think we had better consult my wife. You know she's a very clever woman."

Parker Fillmore

The Three Sisters Who Were Entrapped into a Mountain

There was once an old widow who lived far from any inhabited spot, under a mountain ridge, with her three daughters. She was so poor that all she possessed was a hen, and this was the apple of her eye. She petted and fondled it from morning till night. But one day it so happened that the hen was missing. The woman looked everywhere about her room, but the hen was away, and remained away. "Thou must go out and search for our hen," said the woman to her eldest daughter, "for have it back again we must, even if we have to get it out of the mountain." So the daughter went in search of the hen. She went about in all directions, and searched and coaxed, yet no hen could she find; but all at once she heard a voice from a mountainside saying:

> *"The hen trips in the mountain!*
> *The hen trips in the mountain!"*

She went, naturally, to see whence it proceeded; but just as she came to the spot, she fell through a trap door, far, far down into a vault under the earth. Here she walked through many rooms, every one more beautiful than the other; but in the last a great ugly Troll came to her and asked her if she would be his wife. "No," she answered; she would not on any account. She would go back again directly and look after her hen which had wandered away. On hearing this, the Troll was so angry that he seized her and wrung her head off and then threw her head and body down into a cellar.

In the meantime the mother sat at home expecting and expecting, but no daughter came back. After waiting a long time and neither hearing nor seeing anything more of her, she told the second daughter that she must go out and look for her sister and at the same time "coax back the hen."

Now the second daughter went out, and it happened to her just as it had to her sister; she looked and looked about, and all at once she also heard a voice from a mountainside say:

> *"The hen trips in the mountain!*
> *The hen trips in the mountain!"*

This she thought very strange, and she would go and see whence it proceeded; and so she fell also through the trap door, deep, deep down into the vault. Here she went through all the rooms, and in the innermost the Troll came to her and asked her if she would be his wife. "No." She would not on any account. She would go up again instantly and search for her hen, which had gone astray. Thereupon the Troll was so exasperated that, catching hold of her, he wrung her head off and threw both head and body into the cellar.

When the mother had waited a long time for the other daughter, and no daughter was to be seen or heard of, she said to the youngest: "Now thou must set out and seek after thy sisters. Bad enough it was that the hen strayed away, but worse will it be if we cannot find thy sisters again; and the hen thou canst also coax back at the same time." So the youngest was now to go out. She went in all directions and looked and coaxed, but she saw neither the hen nor her sisters. After wandering about for some time, she came at length to the mountainside and heard the same voice saying:

> *"The hen trips in the mountain!*
> *The hen trips in the mountain!"*

This seemed to her extraordinary, but she would go and see whence it came; and so she also fell through the trap door, deep, deep down into the vault. Here she went through many rooms, every one finer than the other; but she was not terrified and gave herself time to look at this and at that and then cast her eyes on the trap door to the cellar. On looking down she immediately saw her two sisters, who lay there dead. Just as she had shut the trap door again, the Troll came to her.

"Wilt thou be my wife?" asked the Troll.

"Yes, willingly," said the girl, for she saw well enough how it had fared with her sisters. When the Troll heard this, he gave her splendid clothes, the most beautiful she could wish for, and everything she desired, so delighted was he that somebody would be his mate.

When she had been there some time, she was one day more sad and silent than usual; whereupon the Troll asked her what it was that grieved her.

"Oh!" answered she, "it is because I cannot go home again to my mother. I am sure she both hungers and thirsts, and she has no one with her."

"Thou canst not be allowed to go to her," said the Troll, "but put some food in a sack, and I will carry it to her as soon as it is dark."

For this she thanked him and would do so, she said; but at the bottom of the sack she stuffed in a great deal of gold and silver, and then laid a little food on the top, telling the Troll the sack was ready, but that he must on no account look into it. He promised that he would not. As soon as the Troll was gone, she watched him through a little hole there was in the door. When he had carried it a few paces, he said, "This sack is so heavy, I will see what is in it."

He was just about to untie the strings when the girl cried out: "I see you, I see you."

"What sharp eyes thou hast got in thy head," said the Troll and durst not repeat the attempt. On reaching the place where the widow dwelt, he threw the sack in through the door of the room, saying: "There's food for thee from thy daughter; she wants for nothing." And then, mindful of the sunrise, which is fatal to Trolls, he hurried home.

When the young girl had been for some time in the mountain, it happened one day that a goat fell through the trap door. "Who sent for thee, thou long-bearded beast!" said the Troll and fell into a violent passion; so, seizing the goat, he wrung its head off and threw it into the cellar.

"Oh! why did you do that?" said the girl, "he might have been some amusement to me down here."

"Thou needst not put on such a fast-day face," said the Troll. "I can soon put life into the goat again." Saying this he took a flask which hung against the wall, set the goat's head on again, rubbed it with what was in the flask and the animal was as sound as ever.

"Ha, ha!" thought the girl. "That flask is worth something." When she had been some time longer with the Troll, and he had one night gone out, she took the eldest of her sisters, set her head on, and rubbed her with what was in the flask — just as she had seen the Troll do with the goat — and her sister came instantly to life again. The girl then put her into a sack with a little food at the top and as soon as the Troll came home, she said to him: "Dear friend, you must go again to my mother, and carry her a little food. I am sure she both hungers and thirsts, poor thing! And she is so lonely. But do not look into the sack.'' He promised to take the sack and also not to look into it.

When he had gone some distance he thought the sack very heavy, and, going on a little farther, he said: ''This sack is so heavy, I must see what is in it; for of whatever her eyes may be made, I am sure she can't see me now.''

But just as he was going to untie the sack, the girl who was in it cried out, ''I can see you, I can see you.''

''What sharp eyes thou must have in thy head,'' said the Troll, for he thought it was the girl in the mountain that spoke, and therefore did not dare to look again, but carried the sack as fast as he could to the mother. When he came to the door, he threw it inside, saying, ''There is some food for thee from thy daughter; she wants for nothing.'' And then he hurried home.

Some time after this the girl in the mountain performed a like operation on her second sister. She set her head on again, rubbed her with what was in the flask, and put her into a sack; but this time she put as much gold and silver into the sack as it would hold and only a very little food on the top. ''Dear friend,'' said she to the Troll, ''you must go home again to my mother with a little more food, but do not look into the sack.'' The Troll was quite willing to please her and promised he would not look into the sack. But when he had gone a good way, the sack was so insufferably heavy that he was obliged to sit down and rest awhile, being quite unable to carry it any further.

He thought he would untie the string and look into it, but the girl in the sack called out: "I can see you, I can see you!"

"Then thou must have sharp eyes indeed, in thy head," said the Troll quite frightened, and taking up the sack, made all the haste he could to the mother's. When he came to the door of the room, he threw it in, saying, "There is some food from thy daughter for thee; she is in want of nothing." And he hurried home.

When the young girl had been some time longer in the mountain, the Troll having occasion one night to go out, she pretended to be ill and sick, and complained. "It is of no use that you come home until morning," said she to the Troll, "for I feel so sick and ill that I cannot prepare the dinner tonight." So the Troll promised he would not come back.

When the Troll was gone she stuffed some of her clothes with straw and set the straw girl in the chimney corner with a ladle in her hand, so that she looked exactly as if she were standing there herself. She then stole home clandestinely, for she knew that the Troll would not return until daybreak and would never venture after her once the sun had risen.

A little before sunup the Troll returned. "Give me something to eat," said he to the straw girl; but she made him no answer.

"Give me something to eat, I say," said the Troll

again; "for I am hungry." But still there was no answer.

"Give me something to eat," screamed the Troll a third time. "I advise thee to do so; I say dost thou hear? Otherwise I will try to wake thee."

But the girl stood stock still, whereupon he became so furious that he gave her a kick that made the straw fly about in all directions. On seeing that, he found there was something wrong and began to look about, and at last went down into the cellar. Both the girl's sisters were gone, and he was now at a loss to know how all this had happened.

"Ah! Thou shalt pay dearly for this," said he, and he ran out of the house in pursuit of the girl. But in his rage he had quite forgotten himself and the impending dawn, and so he had not traveled far when the sun rose and he burst.

There is plenty of gold and silver still in his mountain, if one only knew how to find the trap door.

Asbjörnsen and Moe